PENGUIN CLASSICS
Death Threats and Other St

'I love reading Simenon. He makes me think of Chekhov'
— William Faulkner

'A truly wonderful writer . . . marvellously readable – lucid, simple, absolutely in tune with the world he creates'
— Muriel Spark

'Few writers have ever conveyed with such a sure touch, the bleakness of human life'   — A. N. Wilson

'One of the greatest writers of the twentieth century . . . Simenon was unequalled at making us look inside, though the ability was masked by his brilliance at absorbing us obsessively in his stories'   — *Guardian*

'A novelist who entered his fictional world as if he were part of it'   — Peter Ackroyd

'The greatest of all, the most genuine novelist we have had in literature'   — André Gide

'Superb . . . The most addictive of writers . . . A unique teller of tales'   — *Observer*

'The mysteries of the human personality are revealed in all their disconcerting complexity'   — Anita Brookner

'A writer who, more than any other crime novelist, combined a high literary reputation with popular appeal'
— P. D. James

'A supreme writer . . . Unforgettable vividness'
— *Independent*

'Compelling, remorseless, brilliant'   — John Gray

'Extraordinary masterpieces of the twentieth century'
— John Banville

ABOUT THE AUTHOR

Georges Simenon was born on 12 February 1903 in Liège, Belgium, and died in 1989 in Lausanne, Switzerland, where he had lived for the latter part of his life. Between 1931 and 1972 he published seventy-five novels and twenty-eight short stories featuring Inspector Maigret.

Simenon always resisted identifying himself with his famous literary character, but acknowledged that they shared an important characteristic:

> My motto, to the extent that I have one, has been noted often enough, and I've always conformed to it. It's the one I've given to old Maigret, who resembles me in certain points . . . 'understand and judge not'.

Penguin is publishing the entire series of Maigret novels.

GEORGES SIMENON

Death Threats
and Other Stories

Translated by ROS SCHWARTZ

PENGUIN BOOKS

PENGUIN CLASSICS

UK | USA | Canada | Ireland | Australia
India | New Zealand | South Africa

Penguin Books is part of the Penguin Random House group of companies
whose addresses can be found at global.penguinrandomhouse.com

Penguin Random House UK

'The Improbable Monsieur Owen' and 'The Men at the Grand Café' first published,
in serial, as 'L'improbable M. Owen' and 'Ceux du Grand Café' 1938
'The Man on the Streets' and 'Candle Auction' first published, in *Maigret et les Petits Cochons
sans queue* 1950, as 'L'homme dans la rue' 1940 and 'Vente à la bougie' 1941
'Death Threats' first published, in serial, as 'Menaces de mort' 1942
These translations first published 2021
001

Copyright © Georges Simenon Limited, 1938, 1940, 1941, 1942
Translation copyright © Ros Schwartz, 2021
GEORGES SIMENON ® Simenon.tm
MAIGRET ® Georges Simenon Limited
All rights reserved

The moral right of the translator has been asserted

Set in 12.5/15 pt Dante MT Std
Typeset by Jouve (UK), Milton Keynes
Printed and bound in Great Britain by Clays Ltd, Elcograf S.p.A.

The authorized representative in the EEA is Penguin Random House Ireland,
Morrison Chambers, 32 Nassau Street, Dublin D02 YH68

ISBN: 978–0–241–48707–5

www.greenpenguin.co.uk

MIX
Paper from
responsible sources
FSC® C018179

Penguin Random House is committed to a
sustainable future for our business, our readers
and our planet. This book is made from Forest
Stewardship Council® certified paper.

Contents

The Improbable Monsieur Owen   1
The Men at the Grand Café   47
The Man on the Streets   93
Candle Auction   115
Death Threats   137

The Improbable Monsieur Owen

I

It was wonderful to be there, eyes closed, feeling his eyelids tingle under the caress of the sun filtering through the yellow curtains; it was especially wonderful to say to himself that it was half past two or three o'clock in the afternoon, maybe later, maybe earlier, and, best of all, that corroder of life, namely a watch, was of no importance.

And that was not all! A number of wonderful things had miraculously come together at that moment. First of all, the panorama, which Maigret couldn't see because his eyes were closed, but he knew it was there within view: the glassy surface of the Mediterranean as seen from Cannes' grand hotels, the forest of shiny masts of the world's most luxurious port to the right and, in the far distance, the Lérins Islands in the blazing light.

Even the sounds that reached Maigret's ears were the sounds of luxury. The car horns were not ordinary horns, but mostly the calls of gleaming, elongated limousines driven by liveried chauffeurs.

This woman who had just had an argument with someone in the neighbouring suite was Viennese, a famous film star. At all hours, there were dozens of autograph hunters waiting for her outside the hotel entrance.

And the rather irritating telephone that rang incessantly in the suite below became forgivable when he learned that the guest in that suite was the prime minister of a major Danubian country.

Maigret was having an afternoon nap! For three days, he'd been staying at a luxury hotel, the Excelsior, on Cannes' Croisette – not to pursue some criminal target or an international swindler, but to enjoy a rest.

A happy chain of circumstances had brought about this miracle, the first being that Aunt Émilie (Madame Maigret had eleven aunts!) was seriously ill in Quimper, with no one to care for her.

'You'll be bored if you come with me. Besides, it's not a good idea since you're barely over the bronchitis you had this winter. Aren't you always telling me that you have a friend in the South who's invited you to stay?'

Maigret's friend was none other than Monsieur Louis.

For ordinary people, Monsieur Louis was merely a doorman in a luxury hotel, dressed in a frock coat decorated with gold-braid keys, and most idiots felt superior to him because they gave him a tip.

Monsieur Louis, however, had his baccalaureate, spoke five languages and had been the manager of a grand hotel in Deauville for many years. But he'd come to the conclusion that the only way to make money in the hotel business was by performing the duties of doorman.

He'd performed them on the Champs-Élysées, in Paris, and that was how, many a time, he'd had occasion to do small favours for Detective Chief Inspector Maigret, then at the Police Judiciaire, and Maigret had done him others in return, such as finding one hundred thousand francs in the cistern of a WC.

'When you come down south . . .'

'Unfortunately that won't be before I retire.'

It had all happened! Maigret was having a nap, like the idle rich. On a chair were his white flannel trousers and at its foot was a pair of snazzy red-and-white shoes.

People came and went in the corridors, chatted, sang, telephoned neighbouring suites; cars drove past in the street and women roasted in the sun; a new government, in Paris, was presenting its programme to Parliament and the Senate, and hundreds of thousands of French people were worrying about the stock markets; the lift went up and down, giving a little click at each floor.

What the hell did all that matter?

Maigret was happy. He had eaten like a horse, drunk like a sailor and soaked up the sun through every pore like a bathing belle.

Aunt Émilie? Well! If she passed away, it was natural at her age, and the only nuisance would be that he'd have to give up these delights to attend the funeral in Brittany where in March the rain was probably bucketing down.

He groaned, peeled his cheek from the pillow and listened to all the sounds that merged into a symphony, with the loudest noise standing out as a solo.

'Come in!' he shouted at last, on recognizing the strange buzz of the doorbell.

Then immediately:

'Is that you, Monsieur Louis?'

'Were you asleep? I'm sorry to disturb you. Something really terrible has happened . . .'

'Would you mind raising the blind?'

Then he could see the sea, as blue as if painted in watercolours, with a white yacht on the horizon and a hydroplane going round in circles, humming like a hornet.

'Would you kindly pass me a glass of water?'

Because his nap, after such a good lunch, had left him with a furry mouth.

'Did you say "terrible"?'

'A murder has been committed in the hotel.'

Monsieur Louis was an intelligent man, distinguished even, with a little brown moustache and a very delicate smile. However, he had not been expecting Inspector Maigret, or rather the former Detective Chief Inspector Maigret, to mutter as if in a dream:

'You don't say!'

'A very mysterious murder.'

Was it drowsiness that made Maigret so indifferent, or was he putting it on in protest against the elegance of his surroundings? In any case, he grunted:

'Go on, tell me if you must . . .'

'It's Monsieur Owen . . .'

'Tell me, Louis, have you called the police?'

'The chief inspector has just arrived. We're expecting the examining magistrate any minute now . . .'

'So?'

'I don't understand you . . .'

'So tell me, Louis: when you happen to be on holiday

and staying at a hotel, do you hand the guests their keys and deliver their post?'

With that, he sat up, his hair dishevelled, hunted for his pipe, filled it, grabbed a blue slipper and had to kneel down to fish the other one out from under the bed.

'I thought you'd be interested,' retorted Monsieur Louis, a little tight-lipped.

'Me? Not at all . . .'

'That's a pity . . .'

'I don't see why.'

'Because I know for a start that the police won't find anything and that you're the only one capable of solving this mystery . . .'

'Well, too bad for the mystery!'

'You haven't even asked me who this Monsieur Owen was . . .'

'I don't care one way or the other.'

'Just as well, because no one knows.'

This time, Maigret, who was trying to grab the ends of his braces, which were dangling down his back, shot Monsieur Louis a roguish glance.

'Well! Well! No one knows?'

'I thought he was Swedish. He looked like it. That's the nationality he gave on his form. You know that, in luxury hotels like ours, we don't ask for our guests' passports, and each person writes what they like. Monsieur Owen's room has been searched but no identity documents were found. The Swedish consul, who lives close to the Excelsior, claims that there was indeed an Ernst Owen, but he died ten years ago.'

Maigret brushed his teeth, picked up his pipe again and ran a wet comb through his hair.

'Why are you telling me all this?'

'No reason! Just think, this Ernst Owen arrived here three weeks ago accompanied by a pretty nurse – one of the prettiest girls I've ever been lucky enough to see – and in our profession, we see plenty!'

Maigret browsed through the six new ties his wife had given him for this trip to find one he liked.

'A blonde with grey eyes. One of those luscious girls with graceful movements, curvaceous but not heavy, a desirable body . . .'

Maigret still didn't want to let on that he was listening.

'The staff would even gossip about them. You know what it's like . . . During meals, we chat . . . The maîtres d' heard this or that . . . The menservants and shoeshine boys chip in with what they know . . . The chambermaids have intimate details . . . In short, this Monsieur Owen and his nurse . . .'

'Was he ill?'

'Not at all! Well, I have no idea. You must have seen him on the terrace without knowing who he was. A lanky gentleman, almost as lanky as King Gustaf, dressed all in grey – a grey flannel suit, grey shirt, grey silk tie, with only a light-coloured panama and white suede shoes. Grey spectacles into the bargain, grey cotton gloves—'

'Gloves?'

'Yes! And that's not all! He would get up at ten o'clock every morning, go downstairs and always sit in the same rattan chair on the terrace, the one under the third umbrella. He'd stay there until one o'clock, his hands resting on his stick, watching the sea in front of him, have lunch and go back to the terrace until five or six o'clock – in other words until it began to turn chilly. Then he'd go back up to his suite, where he was served a cold supper, and was not seen all evening.'

'He was murdered?'

'That's to say that someone was killed in his room . . .'

'So he wasn't the victim?'

'More likely the kill—'

Monsieur Louis decided that Maigret had taken the bait and now he could continue in a less mysterious manner.

'I'm going to tell you the story in a few words. This morning, while I was sorting out the newspapers from Paris, which arrive just before eleven o'clock, I was surprised not to see Monsieur Owen in his usual place. I think I said something to one of the porters. On the off chance, I turned to look at the board and saw that his key wasn't there . . . Anyway! When aperitifs were being served, I went for my little walk around the terrace and again I noticed Monsieur Owen's absence. This time, I went over to reception and asked Monsieur Henry:

'"Is Monsieur Owen unwell?"

'"I don't know."

'At this juncture, let's say between a quarter and half past twelve, I spotted the nurse on her way out, wearing a perfectly tailored pale-green suit. Since she hadn't handed me her key, I didn't have the opportunity to speak to her. I assumed she was going to pick up some medication and I nearly told her that the pharmacies were closed.

'Finally, at two o'clock, the manager of the fourth floor telephoned me to inquire what was happening in room 412. That's Monsieur Owen's suite. The door was still locked and there was no answer. So I went up; I opened the door with my master key and I was quite surprised to find an empty whisky bottle on the table next to a broken glass.

'And then in the bathroom I caught sight of a man's naked body in the bath tub . . .'

'Then what?' Maigret couldn't help asking.

'Then nothing! It wasn't Monsieur Owen.'

'You're saying?'

'I'm saying that it wasn't Monsieur Owen. One of the things my profession requires of me is the ability to recognize faces. I can recall everyone who enters or leaves the hotel. I can confirm that I have never seen that young man . . .'

'I'm sorry! But what about Monsieur Owen?'

'That's precisely where this business becomes extraordinary. His clothes were on the rail and his luggage in the room, with nothing missing. On the other hand, while he clearly couldn't have entered the Excelsior stark naked, there were no items of clothing belonging to him in room 412.'

Maigret stood in front of the vast bay window gazing out at the sea and watching the swimmers' heads bobbing up and down. Monsieur Louis, behind him, told himself that the game was not yet won, and racked his brains for more bait.

'Mind you, as I mentioned, the pretty nurse didn't go out until between a quarter and half past twelve. Now the doctor has just said that the death of the young man who isn't Monsieur Owen occurred first thing in the morning . . .'

'Hmm! Hmm!' grunted Maigret, who was still resisting.

'That's not all. Monsieur Owen seemed to be afraid of having a dizzy spell, or he had other reasons for wanting his nurse close at hand. He'd put her in room 413 with the communicating door between the two suites always open . . .'

'Too bad for her!' sighed Maigret.

'That's what I think. The Flying Squad have already circulated her description widely. They're all the more inclined to believe in her guilt because the testimony of a manservant is categorical. At nine a.m., walking down the corridors and listening at the doors as usual, he clearly recognized the nurse's voice in 412. But at that point, the murder had already been committed.'

Maigret almost wanted, by way of protest at this whole business and against his dreadful hunter's instinct, to put on his swimming trunks and red bathrobe, and then go and lie on the beach and watch the women bathers.

'That's not all,' went on the persistent Monsieur Louis, who, in his austere livery, at times reminded Maigret of a Protestant minister.

'What else is there?'

'I didn't tell you how the young man died.'

'I don't care!' retorted Maigret with a final burst of

energy. 'I'd rather stay in a family guesthouse where I'd pay through the nose and eat veal every day. I've had enough, do you hear, Louis? If I have to pay for my stay by going back to—'

'I'm sorry,' muttered Monsieur Louis humbly, backing towards the door.

He had known Maigret for a very long time. He knew that the latter wouldn't let him leave. Besides, the former inspector was hunching his back, which was always a good sign. And, without turning round, he asked:

'What did he die of?'

Then Monsieur Louis said, in the same tone of voice as if announcing 'Madame's car is waiting':

'He was drowned in the bath!'

His ploy had worked. Maigret had taken the bait.

He'd had to deal with a number of murders and had bent over enough dead bodies to fill a small provincial cemetery.

'If you'd like to come and see—'

'No, Louis! Listen carefully to what I'm about to say: I absolutely insist on being kept out of this investigation. Do you hear? If there is one line about me in the papers, I shall leave your establishment, even though it is most agreeable. Furthermore, I will not deal with any of it . . . I consent to you keeping me updated, informally, while chatting . . . If I have a little idea, which is unlikely, I shan't pretend that I'll refuse to share it with you . . .'

'But you don't want to see the body?'

'They'll photograph it, won't they? Ask the Criminal Records people to give you a print.'

Would he not be left in peace to enjoy the sun and the fragrance of the Mediterranean spring? Alone now, he ferreted around his room in search of something, but he couldn't remember what. He pretended to be in a very bad mood. All the same, when he suddenly encountered his reflection in a mirror, he couldn't help smiling a tiny bit.

'Men like him have a good memory!' he thought.

Such men know what they're doing, moreover, because a Monsieur Louis is well placed to judge a police officer's skill. Well, he hadn't forgotten old Maigret, even though he had retired. The head of the Flying Squad, which had been called in, may well be an ace. Even so, Louis had schemed for a quarter of an hour to secure Maigret's help! And he couldn't have been acting purely in his own interest. The owner of the Excelsior must surely be behind him.

'On condition that I am kept out of it,' he repeated.

Something else made him smile: seeing himself in flannel trousers and a white shirt, with a striped tie that he had chosen without realizing that it was an English university's colours.

'Owen! Owen! All in grey! Grey suit, grey shirt, grey tie. Excuse me! Grey cotton gloves. Ha! Ha! I'd very much like to know why Monsieur Owen wore grey cotton gloves to laze in the sun.'

He no longer heard the telephones, the comings and goings, the discreet click of the lift. A moment later, he went down the stairs for fear of bumping into the official police. He noticed little knots of people in the lobby where the news had leaked out, despite all the precautions.

He walked without stopping past Monsieur Louis, who

was busy at his key rack, and found himself on the Croisette, in an atmosphere so idyllic that it seemed criminal to cause a stir by dying suddenly in the bath tub of a Monsieur Owen.

'Owen... Owen...'

It was the hour when he should write to his wife, and he went to a kiosk and chose a colourful postcard with a picture of yachts, each worth five million francs.

Lovely weather. Sunshine. Had a nap. Life is good! he wrote.

He did not want to give Monsieur Louis the satisfaction of seeing him rush headlong into this case. He forced himself to walk up and down the Croisette three times, not without glancing at the people in swimsuits doing gymnastics on the beach.

'Owen... Owen...'

The name buzzed around inside his head like a trapped fly. But he would have been utterly incapable of saying what bothered him!

'Owen... Owen, let's see...!'

When the sun went down, he had to refrain from walking faster. He acknowledged the greeting of the bellboy by the revolving door and spotted Monsieur Louis deep in conversation with two English guests who needed help fathoming out the railway timetable.

Since Monsieur Louis pretended not to notice that he was waiting and didn't hand him his key, he stood there, pipe in his mouth. He had to listen to a lengthy discussion about the pros and cons of two different trains, then the English guests finally left.

'They've made an arrest!' announced Monsieur Louis.

'Owen?'

'His nurse . . . Just as she was alighting from the railcar in Nice . . . The police called me immediately—'

'What does she have to say?'

'That she knows nothing . . . The inspector will come and fill me in later . . .'

Maigret held out his hand for his key, which was hanging from a chunky white metal star with a number on it.

'That's not all . . .'

'Go on . . .'

'The entire staff was asked to file past the body. No one had ever seen him on the premises. The night porter, my colleague Pitois, whom you know, is categorical. What's more, last night, there was a police officer in the lobby, because of the presence at the Excelsior of the minister, as you know, and he confirms Pitois' statement . . .'

Maigret's hand was still outstretched for his key.

Monsieur Louis pressed him:

'When can I meet you?'

'Why?'

'To pass on the information I'll be receiving later. My shift ends at eight o'clock. There's a quiet bar by the port, the Pétanque . . . If you were to agree . . .'

Some guests were already in dinner jackets. As for Maigret, he preferred to eat in the grill, so as not to have to dress up. The sky was mauve, and so was the sea, in a deeper shade.

'Monsieur Owen . . .' he grunted.

Why hadn't he told Louis to go to hell, instead of tormenting himself as he was doing at present?

Even so, he frowned on reaching his floor and seeing two men transporting a heavy, oblong object, a coffin probably, draped in cloth to make it less sinister. The porters kept a low profile, like thieves, in this hotel where joy and pleasure reigned supreme.

'Monsieur Owen . . .'

The coffin reminded him of his Aunt Émilie, whose death he would be informed of by telegram any time now. Resting his elbows on the balustrade of his balcony, he eventually lit his pipe with a shrug as bursts of the pre-dinner entertainment reached his ears.

'Monsieur Owen . . .'

And his grey gloves! Grey cotton! How odd!

2

'A beer for me . . .' sighed Maigret with satisfaction, emptying his pipe on the floor.

A real beer, at last, in a dimpled glass tankard, and not a little bottle of foreign beer served pretentiously in a crystal glass like at the Excelsior.

At the Pétanque, Maigret was in his element, and suddenly he had that old glint in his eye, both heavy and piercing, for which he was famed at the Police Judiciaire, and the strange placidity that came over him when his mind was working most actively.

Close to him, Monsieur Louis remained very dignified in his black suit, and not a minute went by without someone coming over to greet him or shake his hand, always with a touch of deference. And yet in that bar, at the zinc counter piled with ham baguettes, there were more dinner jackets and tails than blazers, more women in evening gowns than in casual wear; but the dinner jackets were those of the croupiers, the tails with black ties were worn by head waiters, those with white ties by professional dancers, while the pretty women were hostesses at the Casino.

'Any news?' asked Maigret, letting his gaze rove over this little world he knew so well.

'So much news that I made notes on a scrap of paper. Would you like to copy them?'

Maigret shook his head, puffed away on his pipe and appeared to be absorbed by everything that was going on around him, whereas not a detail of what Monsieur Louis was saying escaped him.

'First of all, they haven't been able to identify the victim yet, and his fingerprints, which were wired to Paris, are not in the ledgers of the Palais de Justice. He was a man of twenty-five or twenty-six, in fragile health, who regularly took morphine. At the time of his death, he was still under the influence of the drug.'

'You're not going to claim that this man walked into room 412, stripped naked to take a bath in Monsieur Owen's bath tub, then fainted in the hot water and accidentally drowned?'

'No! They found bruises on his neck and shoulders that were inflicted before he died, by the person who subsequently held the victim's head under water.'

'The time of death, Louis?'

'Let me check . . . Six o'clock in the morning . . . But I learned a strange detail . . . You know the layout of the suites . . . ?

'Next to each bathroom is a private WC . . . These WCs are ventilated by a fanlight measuring around fifty centimetres by fifty . . . Now the pane of the fanlight in room 412 had been removed with a diamond cutter, which suggests that someone got in that way . . . Outside is a fire escape, or rather an iron ladder, that runs close to the fanlight . . . An athletic man could have entered the hotel that way.'

'Again, so as to strip off in Monsieur Owen's room and take a bath in his bath tub!' repeated Maigret, who would not back down. 'A curious idea, don't you think?'

'I'm not trying to explain . . . I'm simply repeating what I've been told . . .'

'Has the young blonde nurse been questioned?'

'Her name's Germaine Devon . . . She really does have a nursing qualification. Before entering Monsieur Owen's employment, she was the live-in nurse for another Swede, Monsieur Stilberg, who died just over a year ago now . . .'

'She knows nothing, of course!'

'Absolutely nothing! She met Monsieur Owen in Paris, in the lobby of a luxury hotel where she'd gone looking for work. He hired her and since then she's gone everywhere with him. According to her, Monsieur Owen was a bag of nerves and scared he was about to lose his mind. Apparently, both his father and his grandfather died insane.'

'And yet he had no personal physician?'

'He was wary of doctors because he was afraid that one of them might have him locked up . . .'

'How did he spend his time, every night?'

'But . . .' exclaimed Monsieur Louis in surprise, re-reading his notes. 'Hold on . . . I don't think anyone asked . . . That would have struck me . . . Presumably he slept . . . ?'

'When does Mademoiselle Germaine – since that's her name – claim she saw her employer for the last time?'

'This morning, she says. She went into his room at around nine, as usual, to take him his breakfast, because he didn't want to be served by the hotel staff. She didn't notice anything unusual. The bathroom door was closed and it didn't occur to her to open it. Monsieur Owen, she states, was as normal, and, while he sat up in bed eating his toast with tea, he asked his nurse to go to Nice for him to deliver a letter that was on the bedside table to a certain address, Avenue du Président-Wilson, if I recall . . .'

'And this letter?'

'Just a minute! So Mademoiselle Germaine took the railcar and was picked up at the station by the police. She had the letter in her bag, or rather an envelope that contained nothing but a blank sheet of paper. As for the address on the envelope, it was non-existent, because Avenue du Président-Wilson does not go up to number 317 . . .'

Maigret signalled to the waiter to serve him another beer and smoked in silence for a good while, his companion not daring to disturb him.

'Well?' he asked, suddenly impatient. 'Is that it?'

'Sorry! I thought—'

'What did you think?'

'That you were busy pondering . . .'

Then Maigret gave a shrug, as if it were stupid to believe he was capable of pondering!

'You're not telling me everything, Louis . . .'

'But . . .'

'I know because you're forgetting to talk to me about a whole part of the investigation . . . Admit that the police asked you which guests had left the hotel since last night . . .'

'That's true . . . Seeing as it didn't lead anywhere, I'd

forgotten about it . . . Besides, you can't really say that it's a departure today, because he notified us last night . . .'

Maigret frowned and became more attentive.

'It was the guest in room 133, Monsieur Saft, a very distinguished young Polish man, who asked me to wake him up at four a.m. He left the Excelsior at five to catch the flight to London . . .'

'Why did you just say that it didn't lead anywhere?'

'The man in the bath tub died at six o'clock . . .'

'Of course, you never saw Monsieur Saft and Monsieur Owen together?'

'Never . . . ! Besides, it would have been difficult for them to meet given that Monsieur Saft spent most of his nights at the Casino or in Monte Carlo, and rested during the day . . .'

'What about Mademoiselle Germaine?'

'What do you mean?'

'Did she go out a lot?'

'I confess I never paid her much attention. If I'd seen her going out at night, I think it would have struck me. In my view, she led a fairly quiet life . . .'

Through the windows, they could see the brightly lit Casino and the white yachts fading in the darkness.

'High stakes?' Monsieur Louis asked a gaming inspector who had just dropped in to the Pétanque for a change of atmosphere.

'Someone's just won a jackpot of a hundred thousand . . .'

Maigret melted into his corner of the banquette, where the smoke was thicker than anywhere else in the café. All of a sudden, he leaped up, banged a coin on the table, paid the waiter and picked up his hat, seemingly not bothered about his companion, who followed him.

His hands in his pockets, he looked as if he had no other aim but to stroll along the jetty, gazing at the silvery, moonlit sea.

'It's much too complicated . . .' he muttered at length, to himself.

'I was under the impression,' said Monsieur Louis tactfully, 'that you had solved much more complicated cases than this one . . .'

Maigret stopped walking, gave him a ponderous look, and shrugged.

'That is not what I meant . . .'

And he resumed his walk and his train of thought. Cars continually pulled up in front of the Casino entrance, and doormen in sky-blue hurried to open the doors. Through the vast bay windows, silhouettes could be seen leaning over the roulette and baccarat tables.

'Supposing . . .'

Monsieur Louis was almost holding his breath, dreading another rebuff. At every moment, he had the feeling that Maigret was about to look up and make a categorical declaration. But no! He would start a sentence, break off, pensive, and shake his head, as if erasing an ill-phrased question from the blackboard.

'Tell me, Louis . . .'

'Yes,' replied Louis at once.

'Would you be able to squeeze through the fanlight in the WC?'

'I haven't tried, but I think I could manage it . . . Admittedly I'm not fat . . .'

'Monsieur Owen wasn't fat either . . . What about the young man in the bath tub?'

'More on the tall, thin side . . .'

'And yet . . .'

What did he mean by 'and yet'? Monsieur Louis walked gingerly, turning around when Maigret turned around, stopping when Maigret stopped in front of some boat which he did not even look at. Monsieur Louis was afraid of only one thing, and that was of hearing Maigret announce: 'Well, having thought about it, I am not going to get involved in this case . . .'

Because he had promised the owner of the Excelsior that his friend Maigret would clear the matter up within a few hours, as he had often seen him do.

'Tell me, Louis . . .'

It was becoming a refrain, and, each time, the doorman trembled.

'Are those fanlights the same throughout the hotel? Mine is of frosted glass. There's a string for opening and closing it, but I've noticed that it's always half-open . . .'

'For ventilation!' explained Monsieur Louis.

'So why did someone remove the pane with a glass cutter? You see that I'm right, that it's too complicated! Now, remember what I am about to tell you: only amateurs make things complicated. A professional job, in general, is neat, with no blunders. Just what is necessary, no more! If Monsieur Owen had wanted to leave the hotel in the morning, he could have done so without any difficulty, via the main door, because the body hadn't been discovered yet. Why the hell has a hole been made in that fanlight?'

'And what if it were to gain entry into the suite?'

Clearly, that day, Maigret was being contrary, because he grunted:

'Then it's too easy . . .'

'I don't follow you . . .'

'I hope not! Otherwise you would be damned good. You have encountered thousands of people at close quarters in your life, but have you often seen someone wearing gloves at all hours of the day?'

'Georges Clemenceau, to name but one . . . He wanted to hide the eczema on his hands . . . I also knew an elderly Englishwoman who was missing a finger and whose glove contained an artificial thumb . . .'

Maigret sighed and looked about him with a truly disgusted expression.

'It's like that envelope containing a blank sheet of paper . . . Listen! Do you want me to tell you what I think?'

Nothing could have delighted Monsieur Louis more, and he beamed.

'Well! I think that if you put an idiot and a very clever man together . . . No! That's not quite it . . . Let's say a professional and an amateur . . . They both have their own little idea . . . They both have a plan . . . They both want to have their say, at all costs, and the result is more or less what you have seen . . . The fanlight in the WC, for example, that's the amateur, because professionals haven't used glass cutters to break in through windows for a long time . . . But the letter to be taken to Nice . . .'

'Do you think the nurse . . . ?'

They were walking past an open bay window from which music blared, and Maigret shot a surly look in the direction of the dancing couples.

'To think that, in the meantime, my wife's aunt . . . I almost wish it were over, that there was a telegram waiting for me at the hotel, obliging me to take the first train to go and lead the mourning in Quimper . . . Have you noticed one thing, at least, you whom I have to thank for all this trouble?'

'You mean . . .'

'No! You haven't even noticed that Mademoiselle Germaine began by working for a Swede . . . To be precise: she was a live-in nurse for a real Swede, who was a genuine invalid and died of his illness into the bargain . . . By the way, what have they done with her?'

'Who?'

'The nurse, for goodness' sake!'

'She's been released . . . Of course, she's still under police surveillance and she's been asked not to leave Cannes . . . For the time being, she must be at the hotel . . .'

'And you didn't say so, you idiot?'

'I didn't know that—'

'Is she still in her suite?'

'Until . . .'

Maigret, turning his back on the jetty, was now striding determinedly down the Croisette. Every now and then, a motionless couple could be seen in the shadows.

'Is there a police officer outside her door?'

'Not exactly . . . He's on her floor and is keeping a watch on her . . . There's another one in the lobby . . .'

This was certainly no time to annoy Maigret, who at last seemed to have an idea and wanted to pursue it to the end.

'Tell me, Louis . . .'

Maigret smiled on hearing himself say those words, which had definitely become a catchphrase.

'What did Monsieur Owen drink?'

'On that matter, I can answer you . . . From my post, I could see him all day long on the terrace, and I noticed that there were only ever bottles of mineral water in front of him . . .'

'What about Mademoiselle Germaine?'

'I don't know. She didn't used to sit on the terrace. Tomorrow I can ask her head waiter and room service . . .'

After all, someone had to have drunk the whisky that had been in the empty bottle found in the room!

'Can you not get me that information before tomorrow?'

'I'll ask the night sommelier . . .'

Which they did. The lobby was empty. A police officer, whom Maigret pretended not to see, was sitting on a crimson velvet banquette reading a newspaper. The night porter greeted his daytime colleague and held out Maigret's key.'

'Call Baptiste.'

A few words exchanged on the telephone.

'Yes . . . Come up for a moment . . .'

Half of the lobby was in the dark, and it was in that half that Maigret went to question the night sommelier.

'Rooms 412 and 413 . . . ? Wait . . . ! No . . . ! I never served them any spirits . . . or rather . . . May I go and get my notebook . . . ?'

When he came back up, he was adamant.

'I never served whisky to 412 or to 413 . . . I've just checked the records and none has ever been ordered during the day either . . . Only mineral waters . . .'

Monsieur Louis was still afraid of seeing Maigret lose heart. It seemed to him that each new piece of information had the effect of making the problem more unfathomable, and he covertly watched the inspector.

'Do you want me to show you to her room?'

'I'll go on my own . . .'

'Shall I wait for you?'

'No! I'll see you tomorrow . . . Keep abreast of anything the police find out . . .'

First he went to his suite, ran a comb through his hair and even wiped his shoes with a cloth to get rid of the dust from the Croisette.

His initial idea had been to knock on the nurse's door, on the floor below his. But, as he was about to go down the stairs, it occurred to him that they would have to speak through the door, which would attract the attention of the Flying Squad officer.

He retraced his steps and closed the window, because the sight of the sea shimmering in the silvery light changed his stream of thought from one moment to the next. On the table, there was a telephone.

Finally he picked up the receiver and heard the hotel operator say:

'Can I help you?'

'Could you put me through to room 413, please?'

He couldn't help feeling a little anxious. He pictured the operator inserting a plug into one of the jacks on the switchboard and announcing:

'Hello! Room 413? . . . I have a call for you . . .'

It must have been more complicated than that, because some time went by and there were several clicks, several muffled calls before a surprised voice asked:

'Who is this?'

Maigret imagined the young woman in bed, perhaps alarmed, who knows? Not having had time to switch on the light.

'Hello!' he said. 'Am I speaking to Mademoiselle Germaine Devon? Good evening, mademoiselle . . .'

'Good evening, monsieur . . .'

She was unnerved, that was certain. She must have been wondering what this caller wanted.

'The person speaking to you has just chanced upon the whisky bottle that was in Monsieur Owen's room this morning . . .'

Total silence.

'Hello! . . . Can you hear me?'

Still silence on the other end of the line, then a click that indicated that the young woman had just found the light switch.

'I know you are still there. And you would be very uneasy if I hung up!'

'Why?'

He had won! The 'why' was full of anxiety. It betrayed a defensive defiance, for sure, but already toned down.

'Perhaps I might be prepared to return this bottle to you . . . But you would have to come and fetch it from my suite . . .'

'Are you staying at the hotel?'

'The floor above yours . . .'

'What do you want of me?'

'To return the bottle to you.'

'Why?'

'Do you not have an idea?'

Once again, a silence, and Maigret's nerves were so tense that his pipe cracked between his teeth.

'Come up to 517 . . . It's just at the end of the corridor . . . A corner room . . . No need to knock . . . The door will be ajar . . .'

Why did the voice ask:

'What should I bring?'

'I see you have understood . . . You know as well as I do what it's worth, don't you? . . . For instance, it would be best not to come to the attention of the police officer watching your floor . . .'

He listened a little longer, hung up, stood there without moving for a good while, his hand resting on the telephone, then he picked up the receiver again, afraid he wouldn't have time to do everything he needed to do.

'Hello! . . .' (He lowered his voice.) 'Operator? . . . Is Monsieur Louis still downstairs? . . . He's just gone out? . . . Yes, room 517 . . . Has he informed you? . . .

'Good . . . This is what I'd like you to do . . . In a moment, room 413 may try to put a call through . . . Can you connect me so that I can listen in? . . . Sorry? . . . Yes . . . If not I'll come down to the switchboard, but it would be better . . . What? . . . Yes . . . Yes . . . I'll wait . . .'

The operator had just asked him to hang up because a call was coming in. A moment later, he called back.

'Hello! . . . Room 517? . . . You were right . . . Room 413 asked me to put a call through to Geneva . . .'

'Are you sure that it was to Geneva?'

'To the Hôtel des Bergues, in fact, because I recognize that number . . . I'll connect you . . . There's a ten-minute wait . . .'

Enough time to fill a pipe and gather up the clothes lying around the room before receiving Mademoiselle Germaine, because Maigret had never learned to tidy up after himself.

3

For the next ten minutes, Maigret would have paid dearly to be able to give a resounding slap to the boy he had been, aged ten, twelve and fifteen, who at school invariably won only three prizes: French composition, oratory and gymnastics.

Somewhere, a distant woman's voice repeated:

'Hello! . . . Hôtel des Bergues, Geneva . . .'

Then, automatically, like on the radio, the voice translated the same words into English and German.

'Hello! . . . Whom do you wish to speak to?'

'Would you put me through to Mr Smith, please?' said a closer voice, which must have been that of Germaine Devon.

And Maigret guessed that the hotel's switchboard operator, whose curiosity he had aroused, was probably listening in too.

With remarkable speed, a man's voice was soon saying:

'Hello! . . .'

Then Germaine Devon, in English, something that Maigret assumed meant:

'Is that Mr Smith?'

More English on the other end, then suddenly an animated conversation, especially on the French side, in a language that was no longer English, but Polish or Russian.

Maigret could only stare resentfully at the carpet. The nurse's voice was emotional, urgent, that of the man at first surprised, and then scolding.

She was recounting a long saga and he interrupted her to ask questions. Then she must have asked what she should do and he became angry and rebuked her for something that completely eluded Maigret.

Looking at the table, Maigret suddenly noticed that an important accessory was missing and, without putting the receiver down, he buzzed for room service.

'Bring me a bottle of whisky as quickly as you can . . .' he ordered, the receiver to his ear.

'Full? With how many glasses?'

'Full or empty! No glasses . . .'

What could she be saying now, in a muted, almost begging tone? A smattering of languages would have been enough to understand the whole thing!

Was the man in Geneva really furious? Sometimes conversations in foreign languages sound that way to those who don't understand, and Maigret was wary. From the intonation, he would have translated as:

'That's your bad luck . . . You'll have to fend for yourself! . . . Leave me in peace! . . .'

But the words spoken could just as easily have meant the opposite.

'Excuse me . . .' someone in the room was saying.

It was the night sommelier asking:

'Which whisky would you like?'

'A square, brown bottle, empty preferably . . .'

'Excuse me?'

'Hurry up, dammit! Can't you see you're going to ruin everything?'

He was hot. He fumed. If he'd kept Monsieur Louis with him, he would at least have been able to translate the telephone conversation.

'Hello! Geneva . . .' said a French voice finally. 'Call over?'

'Call over!' replied Geneva.

'Hello! The Excelsior? . . . Call over? . . . That's three units . . .'

'Thank you . . . Good night . . .' replied the hotel operator.

And the sommelier arrived at last, snooty, with his empty bottle on a silver salver. Maigret barely had the time to get rid of him before there was the sound of footsteps on the stairs. He left the door ajar, turned around on the spot, his hands behind his back, and grunted: 'Come in', as soon as he heard a soft tread on the carpet.

Germaine Devon, a wary look in her eye, was in his room, and he instructed, still with his back to her:

'Please close the door . . .'

Since he had never been any good at languages, he'd had to make up for this deficiency as best he could, so he stood facing the window and turned around only after a lengthy wait, his face as unwelcoming as possible.

'How much did he tell you to pay?' he growled.

'Who?'

'Geneva... How much?'

He had fresh proof of the difference of opinion regarding feminine beauty. Monsieur Louis had described her as:

'An attractive blonde...'

And, because he'd added that she was curvaceous, Maigret had imagined her plump. Mademoiselle Germaine may have been beautiful, but she wasn't pretty. Although her features were regular, they were hard, and her angular shape was far from giving the impression of feminine softness.

'Answer: how much?'

'How much are you asking?'

The bottle was on the table between them. Once it was gone, Maigret would no longer hold any cards.

'It's worth a lot,' he grunted, trying to give himself the hypocritical air of a blackmailer.

'That depends...'

'Depends on what?'

'On the bottle... May I?'

'Just a moment... How much?'

She was tougher than he had initially thought, because he clearly saw suspicion flicker in her gaze.

'I'd like to examine it first...'

'And I'd like to know how much...'

'In that case,' she said, turning towards the door as if to leave.

'If you like!'

'What will you do?' she asked, turning around.

'I'm going to call the police officer who is on your floor. I'll show him this bottle and I'll tell him that I found it in Monsieur Owen's room . . .'

'It's been sealed off . . .'

'I'm well aware of that . . . I will confess, if necessary, that I broke in . . . I will advise the police to analyse the contents, or rather what the bottle had contained . . .'

'And what had it contained?'

'How much?' he repeated.

'And what if it's not the actual bottle?'

'Too bad. Take it or leave it!'

'How much are you asking?'

'A very high price . . . Don't forget the liberty of one or two people is at stake, and probably someone's life . . .'

As he was saying this, he blushed to the roots of his hair with shame because he suddenly realized that he had made an unforgivable mistake. Although he hadn't been able to understand the young woman's conversation, was it not likely that the hotel telephone operator, who was bound to speak several languages, had listened in? He could simply have called him before Germaine Devon's arrival . . .

Too bad! It was too late now! The poker game had begun and he had to play his hand to the end.

'Who are you?' she asked, jaw clenched, glaring at him.

'Let us say I am nobody—'

'Police?'

'No, mademoiselle . . .'

'Colleague?'

'Possibly . . .'

'You're French, aren't you?'

'So are you, I think . . .'

'On my father's side . . . but my mother was Russian . . .'

'I know . . .'

'How do you know?'

'Because I've just listened to the conversation you had with Geneva . . .'

He couldn't help admiring her, because he had never been faced with an adversary who displayed so much composure. She didn't take her eyes off him for a second, and perhaps no one had ever examined his person in such a penetrating, detailed manner. Even her pout said clearly: 'In any case, you're just small fry . . .'

And she contrived to move imperceptibly closer to the table, while Maigret, as if coincidentally, was stepping back from it. When she was just a metre away, her arm shot out and she grabbed the empty whisky bottle, sniffed, and at once her nostrils quivered with such rage that, if she'd had a gun to hand, Maigret reckoned she'd have had his hide.

'. . .'

(Here, a few syllables in Russian, probably, which Maigret couldn't understand but which clearly expressed the young woman's contempt.)

'Is that not the bottle?' he mocked, stepping forward and placing himself between her and the door.

An icy, fearsome look.

'I apologize . . . I must have made a mistake . . . I must

have given back the bottle that contained the substance in question to the sommelier and kept this one . . . I can call him to check . . .'

'What game are you playing? Who are you? What do you want of me? Admit it's not money you're after . . .'

'You have guessed correctly.'

'So? Let me pass . . .'

'Not right away!'

'What have you found out?'

'So far, nothing precise . . . But I'm certain that between us we're going to be able to establish the full truth . . . What did your first employer die of?'

'I won't answer you . . .'

'As you like. In that case, I'm going to ask the police officer to come up and we'll continue the interview in his presence . . .'

'What right do you have?'

'That's none of your business.'

She was beginning to be dismayed by this man who revealed nothing of himself but was gaining a growing hold over her.

'You're not a blackmailer,' she observed, ruefully.

'You're not entirely mistaken. I asked you a question. What illness was Monsieur Stilberg suffering from that meant he needed a nurse by his side all the time?'

At that moment, he wondered whether she would answer him or not. He was playing double or quits, without taking his eyes off her.

'He was a morphine addict,' she murmured, after an inner struggle.

'That's what I thought. He probably tried to kick the habit and hired a nurse to help him?'

'He didn't succeed . . .'

'That's true: he died. But, for a year and a half, you had the leisure of observing the reactions of a morphine addict. Did you already have a lover at that time?'

'Only towards the end . . .'

'What did he do? A student, probably . . . ?'

'How do you know?'

'It doesn't matter . . . He was a student, wasn't he? Chemistry, probably . . . He wasn't well . . . During one bout of illness, he had to take morphine, which is usually the start of addictions of this kind . . .'

It was years since he'd had to put someone through an interrogation like this, nerves tensed, an interrogation where he had to find out everything without ever showing his empty hands. He was hot. He'd let his pipe go out, and he chewed on the stem as he spoke. He paced up and down, missing Quai des Orfèvres, where, when he was tired, he could at least ask a colleague to relieve him.

Luckily, he was spurred on by the thought that meanwhile the officer on duty must be peacefully sleeping on the padded banquette on the floor below!

'You became his mistress . . . You had no job. Neither did he . . . Perhaps his drug abuse prevented him from finishing his thesis?'

'But . . .'

Maigret only had to look at her for confirmation that everything he was saying was absolutely true.

'. . . Who are you?'

'It doesn't matter! It is likely that your lover had to mix in certain circles in Paris to get hold of morphine, and that you went with him . . . Do stop me if I'm wrong . . .'

And he carried on his questioning through sheer doggedness.

'What are you driving at?'

'You met a man whom for the time being we can call Monsieur Saft, which is doubtless not his real name . . . A Pole or a Russian . . . Russian before the war and Polish afterwards, probably . . . Now, if you don't like the name Saft, we can call him Smith and telephone him at the Hôtel des Bergues . . .'

At that point, Germaine sat down, without a word. A simple movement, but how much more significant than all the long tirades! Her legs must be feeling weak. She looked about her, as if seeking something to drink, but this was not yet the moment to give her a break.

'He hauled you over the coals, didn't he, your Monsieur Saft or Smith, during your telephone conversation? And it is your fault, Mademoiselle Germaine! Now, he's a man who knows his profession, an international swindler of some stature. Oh yes he is! Don't protest! He would say to you, if he were here, that, in your situation, you'd better show yourself to be a skilled player. Look! I'll admit that I don't know what his specialism is yet. Was it cheques, bankers' drafts, forged credentials or identity cards? It is of no importance!'

'You're bluffing,' she ventured, recovering a little of her composure.

'What about you? Supposing we're both bluffing . . . At

least I have an advantage over you: you don't know what I know and you don't even know who I am . . .'

'A private detective!'

'You're very warm . . . ! But that's not quite it . . . Monsieur Saft, then, suggests using the acquaintances of your lover . . . What shall we call him?'

She looked brazen:

'Let's say Jean . . .'

Just then, a person in the neighbouring room whom they were keeping awake banged on the wall.

'Let's say Jean . . . And so this Jean, who is sick and addicted to morphine, becomes the centre in fact of an organized gang. He's the only amateur among professionals . . . All he wants is his regular fix and to live a carefree life . . . And this is where you wanted to be cleverer than your accomplices and you made a mistake . . .'

She couldn't stop herself from asking:

'What?'

'You didn't want to be cloistered with your lover in a room in Montmartre or the Latin Quarter . . . Nor did you want to go from one cheap hotel to another . . . You thought it smart to give your Jean a new look and a new identity . . . You had just been the nurse of a Swede . . . so you disguised your friend as a middle-aged Swede like the other one, staying in luxury hotels like him, dressed in grey like him and spending hours and hours in a chair . . .'

She looked away and Maigret went on:

'Those who are unable to create, inevitably imitate . . . You manufactured Monsieur Owen based on Monsieur Stilberg . . . And so your Jean Owen was quite peaceful, warming himself in the sun for most of the day, having his injection at a set time, not without, I am certain, having to do his little job beforehand . . .'

'What little job? Admit you have no idea . . .'

'I admit that I had no idea or almost no idea at the start of this conversation. Relax! Don't look at the door so longingly. You wouldn't even get as far as the foot of the stairs without my telephoning the doorman . . . Three things bothered me, three details that jarred with the rest: the grey gloves, the windowpane removed with a glass cutter and the bottle of whisky . . . Those three details were like the mistakes a pupil adds to the work of the master . . . Let us say that Saft is the expert in question and that you are the pupil . . . Mind you, beginners always want to correct the work of the masters . . .'

He would have given anything for an expertly pulled beer, and even for a whisky, of which there was an empty bottle in front of him, but he couldn't stop in his tracks now. He contented himself with lighting his pipe, which would go out a few seconds later.

'The gloves, that's childish, that's mistake number one. People don't wear gloves all day, including at meals, except to hide damaged hands, and, in this case, it was hard not to think of acid burns . . . The bottle, I didn't think of it until this evening . . . I suddenly remembered that a morphine or cocaine addict is never an alcoholic as well, and that whisky bottle struck me as odd . . . I asked if you drank . . . I was told you didn't . . . I checked that the bottle hadn't been supplied by the hotel . . .'

'Where is it now?' asked the nurse, who was pale but

hadn't lost hope, and was listening to Maigret's explanations with a critical ear.

'It must be in its place, in the room, where no one thought to sniff it... As for the windowpane... I am certain, Mademoiselle Germaine, that your friend Saft or Smith is not proud of you... I'll wager it's an idea that came to you after the event... A painter friend of mine has often said to me that, once he's finished a painting, he has to fight the urge to make one last change, because usually, that change only ruins the painting... Now! Think...'

He took a chair and straddled it and, despite himself, put on a benign air, as if they were talking between professionals.

'Can you see yourself, or can you see your Monsieur Owen, inviting a stranger who has climbed in through the window to strip naked and accept a little morphine jab, then, to round off the party, take off their clothes and have a bath in your bath tub?

'If the windowpane hadn't been removed...! Perhaps certain improbabilities would have been less obvious... but you wanted to spell out the intruder lead too clearly... The same with that letter you had supposedly been asked to deliver by hand to Nice...'

He was stunned to hear her say, just when he least expected it:

'How much?'

'But no, my dear! That was fine earlier, to get you talking. Haven't you understood yet?'

'Twenty thousand...'

'Twenty thousand pounds?'

'Twenty thousand francs ... Forty ... Fifty thousand?'

He shrugged and emptied his pipe on to the rug, which was the first time he had done so since he'd been at the Excelsior.

'No! No! I don't ... Look! You are simply going to tell me whether my little story is correct or not ... Your sick, drug-addict student Jean, since that's how you call him, becomes your lover ... You meet Monsieur Saft, who reveals what you can get out of him ... Then, instead of doing things as they should be done, instead of shutting your student away in some discreet furnished lodging in Paris, you concoct this Monsieur Owen story, this fake identity as a Swede, the wig, the grey attire, the made-up face and, lastly, to hide his damaged hands, those terrible cotton gloves ...

'All that, you see, my dear, reeks of amateurism ... and I am convinced that Saft must have told you so more than once ...

'But you were useful to him, especially Jean Owen, who laundered his cheques or bankers' drafts and must have been adept at imitating signatures ...

'I would wager one hundred to one that you became the mistress of this Saft and that your lover found out ... I'd also bet that he threatened that, if you were unfaithful to him again, he would tell the police everything ...

'And then, you decided to kill him ... Saft shrewdly departed first, leaving the field clear for you. He got off the London flight at Lyon and took the one to Geneva ...

'You created a setting ... You told yourself that the

more baffling the crime, the less chance there would be of your being found out . . .

'First of all, killing your lover, not disguised as Owen, but as his real self . . .

'Now, that six a.m. bath was another mistake! Because who takes a bath at six o'clock in the morning? Someone who rises early or someone who goes to bed late.

'But Monsieur Owen only came out mid-morning and went to bed early.

'What can he be doing in his room until six a.m.? I asked myself.'

She appeared to be resigned. She sat completely still. Her gaze remained riveted on Maigret's eyes.

'. . . Because, whatever you thought, it is not easy to undress a person and then carry them into their bath tub against their will . . . That night, Owen worked as usual . . . Either I am very much mistaken or, to make your job easier, you increased the dose of morphine . . . When he was in his bath, it was easy for you to . . . I don't need to go into detail, do I? A nasty moment!

'Afterwards, you refined your story! More and more! The loud conversation at nine a.m.! The windowpane! The letter to be delivered to Nice! And the wig, the gloves and the cosmetics you took away so as to let people think it was a murder by a non-existent Monsieur Owen . . .

'It's over, mademoiselle!'

He shuddered, surprised himself at those last words, at his tone, because, after several years, he had inadvertently switched to his Quai des Orfèvres voice, that is to say, that of the police chief.

It was so obvious that, instead of protesting, she mumbled, with an instinctive movement to hold out her wrists to be handcuffed:

'Are you arresting me?'

'Me? Not at all . . .'

'So?'

'So nothing . . .'

He was nearly as bewildered as she was by the absurd end of that stormy interview.

'But . . .' began Germaine.

'But what? You don't expect me to arrest you when I am no longer a member of the police?'

'But in that case . . .'

'No! Don't think you're going to get away . . . There is a police officer on the fourth floor and another one downstairs . . .'

'May I go back to my room?'

'What do you want to do?'

With a tragic expression, she replied, looking him in the eyes:

'Can't you guess?'

'Go on!' he sighed.

Too bad! Better for things to end this way! All the same, he did not go to bed but soon went into the corridor to listen. He heard muffled sounds and learned a little later that the young woman had broken the seals on the communicating door with room 412. When he got there, the whisky bottle had disappeared. A police officer had handcuffed Germaine Devon. The night porter was there too.

'Is that what you wanted to do?' asked Maigret, sickened.

She merely smiled.

And, at that moment, he was still unaware what that smile held in store for him, because the investigation lasted six months, and twenty times during those six months Maigret was called as a witness, in the presence of a woman who denied everything, including the evidence.

She still denied it in the criminal court, where Maigret was summoned to appear, and the counsel for the defence almost made him look a fool.

'Some people,' he said, 'cannot come to terms with retirement once and for all, even when the most competent authorities have decided that they have reached the age . . .'

She was nearly acquitted. In the end, the judge gave her the benefit of the doubt and she got off with five years, while Maigret, in a café near the law courts, refused Monsieur Louis' invitation to go and spend a few days in Cannes.

As for Aunt Émilie, she hadn't died on this occasion!

The Men at the Grand Café

I

It had begun in the winter. Once evening fell, Maigret was at a loss as to what to do with himself. He'd barely managed to keep himself entertained for a month, twiddling the knobs on his wireless set, and it took him no longer than half an hour to read three newspapers.

Then he would leave the dining room, where he was in the habit of sitting, and go for a little stroll into the kitchen.

'Haven't you finished yet?' he'd ask his wife. 'What are you doing?'

He went out, came back, went out and came back again, unable to comprehend what work could keep a woman busy in the kitchen all day long, and in the end Madame Maigret had said to him:

'You don't know what to do with your hulking frame. Why don't you play cards with the men at the Grand Café?'

Maigret had resisted for weeks, months almost. Admittedly, he knew everyone in Meung-sur-Loire, where he had retired. He wasn't ashamed of being retired, tending his garden and tinkering in his shack on the riverbank. He sometimes went into the Grand Café, the most modern café, near the bridge, had a beer or, occasionally, a pastis.

Even so, deep down, it felt like a kind of defeat when, at the insistence of Madame Maigret, he sat down at the manille table with its promotional card mat and asked, like a novice:

'What are we playing for?'

'The drinks, as usual . . . Clever devil that you are, you won't often be taking out your wallet . . .'

He had decided to play once, in passing. But the next day, the men sent a boy to let him know that they were waiting for him.

Gradually, he adopted his partners' special jargon, became part of their club and was truly 'one of the men at the Grand Café'. Angèle never asked what they were drinking, she knew in advance. Now he was also one of the men who, when it was time to write down the score, never failed to sigh:

'So, Angèle! Still no tokens . . . ? Do you eat them or what?'

It was a tyranny and in the end he couldn't say whether it was pleasant or unpleasant. In the winter, when the paths were muddy, Maigret gladly put on his varnished clogs to walk to the bridge and, during the grape harvest, then for another month, they drank little bottles of young white wine.

December and January, sometimes February, saw rounds of hot toddies and mulled wine, and spring called for aniseed-flavoured aperitifs, which gave way in summer to the local white wine, served chilled.

'Thirty-six . . .'

'If you say thirty-six, you've got forty . . . I say "little spread" . . .'

'Forty-one . . .'

'To what?'

The other three were on familiar terms, calling each other by their first names or more often by their profession.

'Your turn, butcher!'

The butcher came in his work clothes, sometimes wearing his bloodstained apron. He lost more frequently than the others, got yelled at because he made mistakes, and paid without ever complaining, happy to be there, it seemed, to be admitted to that sacrosanct place, the circle that was the crème de la crème of Meung-sur-Loire.

Sometimes his boy would come to fetch him because a customer needed to speak to him across the road, in his shop whose red shutters were visible from the café. He always found someone to hold his cards for him, and the others would take advantage of it to add points to his score or play some other trick on him.

'Your turn, Citroën . . . !'

That was the mechanic, who took the game seriously and always won, but was harsh when a partner made a mistake.

The third of those who could be described as the mainstays was Maigret, whom they all called inspector and only dared to tease timidly.

The fourth player was interchangeable. When the mayor, who was a vet, didn't show up, Urbain, the owner of the Grand Café, took his place, unless the farrier happened to be there.

At five minutes to five, the butcher was to be seen standing in his doorway, waiting for the signal. Maigret would arrive, sucking his pipe, his hands thrust deep in his pockets.

Opposite the Grand Café was another, the Commerce, more cramped and darker, which made it a second-class establishment too unremarkable to ever appear in the local news.

'Go and fetch your father, boy . . . Tell him we're waiting for him . . .'

And the farrier's, or the mechanic's or the vet's kid would leave his friends for a moment to go and shout at his door:

'Papa . . . ! The men at the Grand Café want you . . .'

'Tell them I'm on my way . . .'

There was talk of politics, of course, but only after the game, when it finished early, or when the butcher won and was called a *fascist*.

As for women, there were none to speak of. The owner's wife, Madame Urbain, was sad and pale as a leek, always busy with countless medicinal cures for her digestion, and confiding details of the functioning of her organs to anyone and everyone, which people found off-putting.

Then there was Angèle, the waitress, who was twenty.

'A pretty little dish,' the mechanic had said to Maigret, 'but Urbain keeps an eye on her . . .'

'Ah! He's . . .'

'Shhh . . . !'

Was it true? Wasn't it true? Maigret had taken no notice and he didn't agree with the mechanic. He found Angèle to be a determined-looking young woman with shifty eyes. But the others were probably only interested in the particularly buxom contents of her blouse.

During the game, people came in for a drink and sat behind the players for a while, nodding their heads in approval or shaking them in disapproval, but, all things considered, they were just small fry.

'The men at the Grand Café' were the four or five manille players, the men for whom, from half past four, tables were wiped and for whom, every two weeks, because Maigret had once remarked that the cards were sticky, the owner bought a new deck with gilt corners.

Was it possible to imagine that, in such a haven of French rural tranquillity, Maigret would find himself at the heart of a drama, not in a professional capacity and not even, as had happened in the past, accidentally and from a distance?

And just imagine his situation, as a former detective chief inspector of the Police Judiciaire, when the news spread throughout the town:

'One of the men at the Grand Café has committed a murder!'

It was in April, the sun was still shining in the street and on the bridge when the card game started, and it was dark when it ended.

It must have been at the beginning of the month,

because the butcher had gone to the Vendée the day before and come back that same evening. Once a month, he would go to Luçon. He had explained – and Maigret hadn't taken any particular interest in the ins and outs of butchering – that he leased some marshland in the Vendée for fattening up animals, which he bought scrawny . . .

The fact remains that he had alighted from his van, because he only ever drove around in a van. He was wearing, as he always did on all these trips, his hunting outfit, with brown leather boots and corduroy plus-fours over which nothing would have stopped him wearing his butcher's apron.

It was only after the event that people recalled those tiny details, because in the heat of the moment no one thought anything of it, given that it was an evening like any other, with a pretty sunset over the sandbanks of the Loire.

But Maigret remembered having said to himself: 'Odd that he doesn't pop into his shop for a moment . . .'

Because, through the bow windows of the Grand Café, you could see, almost opposite, the shutters and marble counters of the butcher's shop, where the butcher had not set foot on alighting from his van.

It was the period of aniseed-flavoured aperitifs, which Angèle served everyone without asking, except for the farrier, who drank Vittel with strawberry cordial all year round.

The vet was there, short, bearded and moustachioed, all a-fidget, complaining like no one else when he lost and instantly lewd when the conversation turned to women.

He was the only one to make suggestive remarks aloud to Angèle, which seemed to confirm the farrier's theory. Maigret had noticed that when that happened, although Urbain's commercial instinct made him bite his tongue, he was still aggrieved.

In short, the players were paired up, after some dithering as to who would partner whom.

'Play!' the mayor-cum-vet said to Urbain.

'No way! You play!' answered the owner of the Grand Café.

The wireless was on in the background, but it was so much part of the atmosphere that no one was listening. The Urbains' son, aged two, was crawling about near the stove, and Madame Urbain, more out of sorts than ever, was embroidering a cushion for her sitting room, where no one ever set foot.

'Thirty-six . . .'

'Thirty-seven . . .'

'Fifty-six . . .'

The setting sun slanted in, illuminating the ginger hairs on the face of the mayor-cum-vet, and Maigret mused that the little man could have made a very presentable faun.

'If he were a doctor, I wouldn't send my wife to him' was one of the thoughts going through his mind.

Next to him was the butcher, taciturn and probably tired from his trip, because he'd had bad weather in the morning. Besides, he was worried, which he didn't keep to himself for long.

'I have to go and see the notary . . .' he announced while playing.

'Tonight?' retorted the farrier, whose skin was speckled with black. 'Do you think he'll wait for you?'

'I'll go to his home . . . I have before . . . I don't like keeping money in the house . . .'

'That's clever! If you'd played the seven of hearts instead of the ace of clubs, I'd have got rid of my ace of diamonds and he'd have been done for . . . Angèle . . . !'

She came over. No one paid any attention.

'Bring me an ice cube, would you?'

Urbain was sitting just behind Maigret, as usual, and since he could see two players' hands, he was constantly shaking his head in disapproval.

'You, stop giving the game away . . .'

'Never, mayor . . .'

Had they even heard the butcher's words? Gradually, as the tokens (they'd had to ask for counters, as they did every night!) piled up in front of the players, the air turned blue, then the lamps were lit, and the street through the windows was nothing but a black hole, although one light bulb could be seen, that of the butcher's shop.

'What do you want the notary for? Are you after Jules' house?'

'Why? Are you?'

'Not me . . . But I know someone . . .'

Maigret, who was privy to what they were talking about, was still taking no interest in the conversation. He hoped to achieve a grand spread, which he was a lot more excited about.

'Do you know what the Belgian plans to do with it?'

'I heard something about it . . . A cinema . . . !'

'Gentlemen, back to the game,' protested the farrier, who had called forty-six.

'Grand spread!' Maigret ventured at last.

He'd done it. This was the first time he'd managed it in months.

'Five points each,' he said to the others.

'Is it true you're keen to buy it?' repeated the vet.

'Not at all . . .' sighed the butcher, slightly embarrassed.

'You should tell me if you are . . . I promised the Belgian there'd be no bids . . . It's in everyone's interest to have a cinema . . .'

The game resumed. Maigret thought he saw the pharmacist and the doctor come in to play billiards in the other room, but they never stopped to mix with the manille players.

'Twenty-six!'

'If you're passing, I'll pass . . .'

They threw down their cards. Angèle served the second round, because it was a ritual to drink two rounds, since they played two games. Why, as she leaned over the table, did Maigret look at Urbain? And why did he have the impression that the latter was sad, as if after a lovers' tiff?

'Of course!' he said to himself. Yesterday had been Angèle's day off and she'd been to Orléans again. If he really was her lover, he must be jealous of her weekly outings . . .

Another game! There was no time to think. Just that aniseed taste in his mouth from the aperitif and one pipe after another.

Madame Maigret was admirable – she needed no one to be happy and was able to spend the entire day in her kitchen or doing her laundry, alone with her thoughts! But did she actually think?

Now, now! He didn't want to be unkind. But there were days, like this one, when the atmosphere of the Grand Café was particularly gloomy and when he felt like a dog on a chain. Had he left Quai des Orfèvres to come and play cards with these good fools? They didn't even give him five minutes' respite and, if he was late, that horrid kid with a shrill voice – the son of the vet, a redhead like his father – came and yelled at the garden gate:

'The men at the Grand Café are waiting for you . . . !'

Here we go! Already he had no more good cards! He never did have a decent hand! Apart from his grand spread . . .

'What is it?' Urbain asked his wife, who was calling him.

And he went over to her. They spoke in hushed voices. Maigret thought that poor Urbain had married a very unpleasant woman, although his affair with Angèle, if he was having one, couldn't always be much fun.

But that's life in the provinces, when you take the narrow view, be it in the Loire, the Cher or the Rhône. Only tiny details change.

In the South, Maigret would have been playing boules and in Lille, skittles . . .

'You've lost, my friend!' said the mayor, rising and wiping his moustache, which was always damp, like that of a Barbet dog.

As for saying exactly in what order they left . . . The butcher and Maigret were the two losers. Maigret had gone over to the bar, where he'd counted his change and given Angèle a one-franc tip . . . The others only gave ten centimes, but, since he had got into the habit, too bad . . .

One detail, however . . . When he came to pay, the butcher had first of all taken out his wallet, showing how fat it was, so fat that one-thousand-franc notes were sticking out, and had complained:

'You see, I must go to the notary's . . .'

The doctor and the pharmacist, both of them young, one fair-haired and the other dark, were still playing billiards and, in the evenings, they would meet up with their wives to play bridge.

'Good night, inspector!'

'Good night, everybody . . . !'

What else . . . ?

Maigret walked along the dark street, his hands in his pockets. There was still a light on inside the grocer's, but the lamps in the window displays were switched off. He had to follow the street until the third gas lamp, then turn right. He was almost there when the butcher drove past him, stopped and waited.

It was utterly out of the ordinary. Maigret thought the butcher must have something he wanted to tell him.

'Do you think I can call on the notary when his office is closed?'

'Well . . . Given that he knows you . . .'

'Very well . . . ! Good night . . .'

Maigret remembered it well. The van was painted a

mottled green. He saw the rear light fade into the night. Meanwhile, he turned right, as usual, and was soon pushing open his front door with a familiar gesture and sniffing, as he did every evening, the aromas of food cooking.

There was wild rabbit, which was rare at that time: a landowner in Cléry had organized a beat the previous day to exterminate the hundreds of rabbits that were causing serious damage.

'Did you win?'

'I lost.'

'Don't you think you lose more often than is fair? Might the others be cheating?'

Dear Madame Maigret, who was suspicious even of the men at the Grand Café!

'Of course not . . . Not to mention that it costs me exactly four francs fifty every evening . . .'

'So long as you're having fun for your money . . .'

That was the point. He wasn't having fun, but he couldn't have explained it to her. It had become a compulsion, a necessity, in other words a need that came over him at a set time and of which he was close to feeling ashamed, like a cocaine addict or an inveterate drinker.

'Any news?'

'None . . . When we play, we barely speak . . .'

'Do you know what I've heard?'

'How would I know?'

'That Angèle, the little waitress at the café, was pregnant and that she got rid of it . . .'

'I didn't notice anything . . .'

'Of course not! It's not even three months . . . She told the pharmacist's maid who . . .'

After the wild rabbit and the frangipane tart (one of Madame Maigret's specialities), he read the local newspaper and the Paris newspaper, sitting in the same armchair as he had for three years now, beside the stove, even in summer when it was not alight.

All of a sudden, like a thunderclap, the narrow street was full of people, voices, there was someone thumping on the door, banging the knocker.

'Inspector . . . Quick . . . ! Inspector . . . !'

It was the farrier, the man who only drank strawberry-flavoured Vittel and who, that evening, seemed drunk. He was with people Maigret knew by sight, and children were weaving in and out of the adults' legs.

'The butcher's been killed!'

'What?'

'You must come . . . The mayor's phoning the gendarmerie . . .

'His van was found by the side of the road, with a burst tyre . . . And he'd been shot in the chest . . .'

'But where . . . ? Where did it happen?'

'Just outside Meung . . . A few minutes, for certain, after he left us . . . The coal merchant noticed the van when he was driving past in his truck. The headlights were still on . . . He took the butcher home . . .'

'Of course!'

In other words, everything had already been touched. But, as Maigret was about to get angry, he felt a jolt of rebellion.

'This is none of my business . . . You say you've informed the gendarmerie . . . ?'

'Don't you understand?'

'What don't I understand?'

'Don't you remember what he told us this evening, about what he had in his pocket . . . People will say . . . They'll claim . . .'

Naturally! They would investigate the regulars at the Grand Café, it was inevitable! And there weren't many of them!

'What about you, when did you see him for the last time?' asked the farrier.

'Just before the crossroads . . . He stopped for a second . . .'

'Did you speak to him?'

'He spoke to me . . .'

'Oh . . . !'

No! Not that! It was already enough that a murder had been committed in Maigret's immediate circle, but they'd better not start suspecting him!

'Please come . . . Everyone's at sixes and sevens . . . His wife claims it was a trap . . .'

'What trap?'

'She won't say . . .'

Maigret fetched his hat and, since he couldn't find the old fedora he wore in the country, he put on his bowler hat, which was sort of symbolic.

'I'll be back in a minute!' he promised his wife as he used to do in the old days, when he left for an investigation that sometimes kept him away for a week.

She understood so well that she advised:
'Don't forget your key...'
'No need... I'll be back...'

He felt silly, walking in the street with the farrier on his left, surrounded by ten, fifteen onlookers, not to mention the horde of brats. The better informed kids explained:

'He's an ex-policeman... He'll be doing the investigation... Just wait...!'

In the main street, there were shadows on the pavements, on the doorsteps, a gathering outside the butcher's shop, opposite the Grand Café.

'Look! Here come the gendarmes...'

And indeed, three of them had arrived, on a motorbike and sidecar, and, emboldened by their uniforms, they dismounted purposefully in the midst of the bystanders.

2

Madame Maigret did not understand. She had been surprised when Maigret had returned barely half an hour after they had come to fetch him.

'What's wrong . . . ? Is it over?'

'No! But I don't want to be involved.'

He was unpleasant, grumpy. He twiddled the knobs of the wireless absent-mindedly.

'Was he killed by someone who robbed him?' asked Madame Maigret, busy sewing.

'His money has gone, yes!'

'Did he have a lot on him?'

'So they say . . .'

She thought that Maigret was upset by the tragic death of a companion with whom he'd been playing cards a few moments earlier. There was an element of that, of course. But there was also, and more importantly, the things that the former police inspector instinctively knew.

Earlier, the people from the Grand Café, the onlookers, everyone in other words, had been stunned to hear him declare, not like someone who wants to be persuaded otherwise, but like a man whose mind is made up:

'I will not be involved in the case in any way.'

They were all still talking about it down there. They were probably waiting for the chief of the Orléans Flying Squad. Maigret knew nothing, didn't want to know anything. He retired to bed even though it wasn't yet ten o'clock. At around eight o'clock the next morning, he went downstairs in his slippers, unshaven, and poured himself a bowl of coffee.

'Aren't you going to see if there's any news?'

'No!'

He contented himself with collecting the local newspaper from the letterbox.

> ... the card game between our town's prominent citizens was coming to an end ... among them was our distinguished mayor ... Inspector Maigret, an ace of the Police Judiciaire ...

And some kind words for each one:

> ... the Grand Café, which is our town's exclusive meeting place ... the victim, whose honesty and devotion were universally appreciated ... the gendarmerie, under the leadership of the highly esteemed Lieutenant de Velpeau ... the arrival of Chief Inspector Gabrielli, whose intuition and shrewdness ... Doctor Dubois, always on the go when it's a matter of ...

'Any developments?' inquired Madame Maigret.

Nothing new, nothing old! Nothing at all! A column to explain that the butcher had been murdered when he was no more than a hundred metres from the notary's house.

He'd been shot in the chest after a burst tyre had forced him to stop his van.

That was all. His wallet had been found in his pocket, empty. The gun had been left by the roadside, a high-calibre cylinder revolver.

Seeing Maigret heading for the fishing shack, his wife asked in surprise:

'Are you going fishing? But what if, in the meantime . . .'

She wanted to add: 'What if you're needed?'

And, just at that moment, there was a knock on the door. Maigret grunted and looked even gloomier on recognizing from a distance the butcher's wife, who was already wearing a black dress, but not yet a crêpe armband.

Madame Maigret showed her into the dining room and came to fetch her husband.

'She wants to speak to you in private . . . You should put on your other slippers . . . Those are old and tatty.'

The butcher's wife waited until the door was shut, cleared her throat, wiped her nose with her handkerchief and looked Maigret in the eyes with the instinctive suspicion of a shopkeeper.

'I need your advice . . .' she began. 'I know you were a friend of my husband's . . . I presume he confided in you . . .'

'No, madame. I can assure you that your husband never told me the slightest thing.'

'Well . . . ! You saw him every day, you must have watched him and—'

'There's no point saying any more, madame. I swear to you that I didn't watch your husband. True, we played cards, but that was as far as our friendship went . . .'

'You don't want to tell me anything? That's it, isn't it? What about when you realize that I know? I didn't only find out today, or yesterday, believe me! He was absolutely crazy about that girl. I saw him change in front of my eyes. Listen! In the end, he almost took a dislike to our boy, had no patience with him, and, last Sunday, he thrashed him for some trifling reason, he'd become so irritable—'

'Excuse me, madame . . .'

'Let me finish . . . I could have made a scene, stopped him from going to the café and seeing that girl . . . I chose to keep quiet, to mope alone, in the hope he'd get over it . . . On Mondays, I would see Angèle set off for Orléans and I knew for sure that my husband's van wasn't far away, that he'd come back in the evening in a better mood than on other days . . . So I have come to ask you—'

'I repeat, madame, that I know nothing, absolutely nothing, and I don't want to know anything. The police have opened an investigation. The prosecutor is expected this morning . . .'

'He's already been . . .'

'In that case, you see that . . .'

He couldn't brutally ask her to leave, and she was clinging on to some hope or other.

'I would have thought that, in such circumstances . . .'

'But, madame, please understand that I am powerless. There is an official police force, the investigation will follow its course and will inevitably reach the right conclusion . . .'

When he was finally able to close the door behind her, he said:

'And I've made another enemy!'

'Why do you refuse to investigate this murder? I understand that woman a little, I do . . .'

Tough! He had his reasons, and made his way to the bottom of the garden, not with the intention of going fishing, but simply to sort out his tackle.

He didn't need to venture into town to know what was happening there. He imagined the butcher's wife returning home, walking through the groups of bystanders; and the to-ing and fro-ing in the Grand Café opposite, which would be full of people all day long.

What's more, it was market day. The street was blocked by the farmers' carts, and calves were led past on ropes, women carried live chickens by their feet.

The butcher was dead! His family arrived from Amboise, his home town. Red eyes, moist kisses, a scent of flowers, burnt wax, and children no one knew what to do with on a day like this, not daring to send them out to play in the street.

When the door knocker clanged, Maigret merely looked up, glanced out from the shack's doorway and sighed:

'Next . . . !'

Because they would all come, he was certain! He'd have done better to go fishing and spend the day on his boat, on the edge of the current. Otherwise, how could he stop them telling him secrets he didn't want to hear?

This time, it was the mayor, whom Maigret did not receive in the dining room, but in the shack, where at least he could keep busy while listening.

'I thought we'd be seeing you this morning,' said the

short man, 'so, thinking you were ill, I came to inquire after your health . . .'

Oh yes! What could this one want? Was he also going to talk about the butcher's love life?

'Naturally, since last night, your mind must have been working . . . Don't deny it, inspector! A man like you can't witness a tragedy of this kind without trying to figure out certain problems, whether you want to or not . . . It's like me when I'm in front of an animal . . . I unwittingly make a diagnosis . . . By the way, do you know Michel, the farrier's son?'

Maigret was painstakingly attaching a sinker to a fishing line, seeming even more absorbed than usual.

'As mayor, I have had several occasions to be concerned about him . . . I assume that professional confidentiality doesn't apply to us . . .'

'Oh yes it does! Oh yes it does!' retorted Maigret gravely.

'But I can tell you, since it is common knowledge, that he's a hothead and has given his father endless trouble. He's twenty-three now and has still never had any kind of serious occupation . . . He's been in Meung for a few days . . . Apparently in Paris he was unemployed . . . And lastly, I must add that he has already been convicted for assault and battery . . . On that subject—'

'Goodbye, mayor . . .'

'Admit that you're not thinking about your fishing rods at the moment, but that your mind . . .'

Whatever next? Was it because this Michel had waved a knife around at a local festival that he'd gone and murdered the butcher on the road?

The strangest thing was that, left to his own devices for half an hour, Maigret grew impatient, without wanting to admit it to himself, and he was listening out for the door knocker. He was like those petulant children who refuse to play with the others but can't help watching them running around with envy.

Why wasn't he down there, at the Grand Café, like everyone else? And why this act, why pretend to be furious when someone brought him news?

It was almost midday when there was another knock and, this time, Maigret found himself face to face with a man he thought he recognized but couldn't quite place.

'We worked together once, on a forged passport case . . . I was just an inspector then . . . Allow me to introduce myself: Detective Chief Inspector Gabrielli . . .'

'Pleased to meet you . . . A glass of white . . . ? Come and sit in the sun . . . It's not warm enough yet to stay in the shade . . .'

'I expected to meet you at the scene, but I was told that you were fiercely barricaded in at home . . . Tell me! Don't you find this business strange? All morning I've been questioning people . . . But all I've managed to find out is that the butcher was in love with Angèle, the waitress at the Grand Café . . . So I inquired about her . . . She's a girl who had a very unhappy childhood, because her father is a drunkard of the worst kind . . . I said to myself that perhaps this girl had some dubious friends . . . She might have had a young thug for a lover and . . .'

'Cheers!'

'Am I boring you? Of course, you were there, you know all this . . .'

'I assure you,' sighed Maigret, 'that I know absolutely nothing. The butcher is dead, and I'm sorry about that, like everyone else . . .'

'You have a strange way of saying it . . .'

'Cigar . . . ? A pipe . . . ?'

'Well . . . ! I can see you don't want to talk . . . When I heard you were here, I thought my job would be much easier . . .'

Madame Maigret, who was shuttling between the garden and the kitchen, where she had a stew on the stove, kept darting anxious glances at her husband. She had never seen him like this. He was a little bit like the Maigret of the bad days in autumn, when he was coming down with flu and out of sorts.

'In short,' concluded Gabrielli, 'I didn't find out anything on that front. And I can't suspect the mayor, or you, or the farrier! I've commissioned various expert reports, including one on the revolver, but I don't have high expectations because it's an old gun and there are so many of them lying around in the countryside. A vagrant? That's what we always say when we can't find anything, and the gendarmeries will make it their business to give all the drifters a rough time . . .'

He was still hopeful, waiting for Maigret finally to make up his mind and open his mouth. But no! Maigret wasn't budging, wasn't even curious enough to question him!

Madame Maigret, however, gave him a helping hand by coming in to inquire:

'Will you join us for a simple lunch, inspector? I've got

a mutton stew and baby asparagus that a relative sent me from the Île de Ré . . .'

It would have taken some daring to accept this invitation, made in defiance of Maigret's surly air. He certainly wasn't going to any great lengths to be hospitable!

'Strange fellow . . .' said Gabrielli to himself as he walked off empty-handed. 'Does he know something? Is it old age that makes him like that . . . ? Provincial life . . . ?'

And Madame Maigret, who rarely scolded her husband, took the liberty of chiding:

'You were barely polite to that young man. I don't know what's the matter with you, but I was embarrassed for you . . .'

He didn't bother to reply and poured himself a third glass of white wine.

Was this what he'd been waiting for all morning, and was the wait the cause of his ill humour? In any case, when he heard Angèle's voice asking Madame Maigret whether Maigret was at home, he stood up, opened the door and immediately said:

'This way . . . Come in . . . Close the door . . .'

He had shown her into the dining room and left his wife in the kitchen. He smoked his pipe, paced and offered his visitor a chair.

'I couldn't come any sooner . . .' she began. 'I was sort of hoping that you'd come and that I'd find a way of talking to you for a moment.'

She was calm. Now she appeared to be waiting for the questions that Maigret was bound to ask her, but he sat carefully scratching at a little spot of paint on his sleeve.

'The police haven't asked me anything . . . But I thought to myself that you, who live here, would definitely know about it. I came so you could tell me what to do . . .'

'About what?'

'The butcher . . . ! You knew, didn't you, that he was chasing after me? Even though it caused me scenes with Monsieur Urbain almost every day . . . On Mondays, he'd got into the habit of following me, in Orléans . . . He wasn't a bad man . . . On several occasions he cried in front of me, and that's what made me give in . . .'

God knows Maigret wasn't encouraging her to continue confiding in him! But nothing could stop Angèle, who felt the need to go into detail.

'Monsieur Urbain got to know that I went to a hotel with the butcher twice . . . He told me I had to choose . . . I found myself in an awkward situation, because Hubert (the butcher) wanted to leave his wife, his business and his kid to run off with me . . . What would you have done in my shoes?'

Did she hope he was going to reply, into the bargain? Wasn't it enough to have to listen to all that?

'A few days ago, he made the decision to do it . . . He wrote me several letters . . . He told me that he'd had enough, that he couldn't carry on living like this and that, if I didn't go off with him, he'd kill himself . . . That's what I should have said, isn't it . . . ? That letter, where he talks of suicide, is from the day before yesterday . . . Should I tell the police about it? Should I talk about Monsieur Urbain, at the risk of . . . But people do need to know that he killed himself . . .'

She wasn't crying but merely sniffing and staring contritely at the floor.

'I thought you'd advise me . . . Monsieur Urbain has his suspicions . . . Since this morning, he's been hovering over me nonstop, wondering what I'm going to do . . . He's so jealous that I'm always afraid he'll do something dreadful . . .'

Maigret went and emptied his pipe into an ashtray.

'I have nothing to say to you . . .' he muttered after a lengthy silence.

'Don't you believe me? Maybe you think I'm making it all up? Here! I've brought the letters to show you . . .'

She fished out from her bag some pathetic, crumpled letters written on cheap grocery-shop paper. Maigret waved them away.

'Read! Now that he's dead, it doesn't matter any more . . .'

'There's no point . . .'

'Don't you believe that he committed suicide?'

'It makes no difference!'

'Do you think he was killed by someone wanting to rob him? Tell me! Is that what you think?'

'I don't think anything, my poor Angèle . . .'

'Why "poor"?'

'No reason . . . ! Forgive me for not being able to advise you . . . Do as you see fit . . . Follow the voice of your conscience, as they say . . . As far as I'm concerned, I've already forgotten what you have told me . . .'

She straightened up, pale and on edge.

'I don't understand you . . .'

'That is of no importance.'

'It's as if you suspect me, when . . . Is that it? Do you suspect me of killing the butcher?'

'You were at the café when he died, weren't you?'

'And if I hadn't been at the café, you would have thought . . .'

He sighed. The minutes, the seconds felt never-ending. He wondered whether he would manage to keep up the placidity he was renowned for much longer.

'Please leave, Angèle . . . It would be better . . . I know nothing . . . I don't want to know anything . . .'

'Very well!'

She went over to the door and left, utterly confused. She turned around, once in the lane, convinced that he'd call her back. As for Madame Maigret, she asked with a cunning look in her eye:

'Is that her?'

'Her, who?'

'You know very well what I mean . . .'

'Not at all!'

'Come on, admit there's a reason why you're being the way you are today . . . I've known you long enough to tell that you're not your usual self . . . Already, last night, when you came in . . .'

'What did I do?'

'Nothing! But you had that expression on your face . . . ! Something's bothering you or upsetting you . . .'

'That's quite natural, isn't it?'

'Why don't you go outside like everyone else? You don't normally stay here all day long . . .'

'I don't want everyone talking to me about the butcher . . .'

'About the butcher, or that girl?'

'Silly fool . . . !'

'Thank you . . . !'

They actually almost had an argument, something that hadn't happened for years. Maigret was going round in circles like a sick animal.

'When is the funeral?' his wife came to ask him as he was tidying away his old newspapers.

'I don't know.'

'Will you go?'

'I have to . . .'

'Won't you tell me why that girl came here?'

'No!'

'Are you expecting anyone else?'

'I'd rather no one came. Unfortunately, more people will come. They're all determined to tell me their secrets . . .'

'You don't usually complain about that . . . Don't you think you should have a shave?'

He shaved, out of idleness, and changed his clothes and slippers. He wasn't quite ready when the knocker announced a new visitor. He leaned over the bannister and recognized the voice of Urbain, who was saying:

'Don't disturb him . . . I'll wait . . . By the way, has Angèle, my little waitress, been here?'

And trusty Madame Maigret, keen to say the right thing:

'I don't remember . . . The thing is, I don't know her by sight . . .'

'A small, thin girl, dressed in black . . .'

'I don't think so . . . No . . . But my husband will be able to tell you for certain . . .'

Maigret shrugged and even gave a faint smile. He finished dressing, opened the window and paused to fill a pipe and gaze at the Loire, the breeze gently ruffling its waters and making little wavelets.

Eventually, he made up his mind to go downstairs, went into the dining room and closed the door.

'Good afternoon, inspector . . . Forgive me for disturbing you . . . But, if Angèle has been to see you, I'm sure you'll understand . . .'

Urbain was pale, his gaze racked with anxiety, nervous hands tugging at the rim of his hat.

'Do sit down, please . . . A little glass of white wine . . . ? Aren't people waiting for you back at the café?'

Urbain shuddered.

'What do you mean?'

'Nothing . . . That it's market day . . . That there must be a lot of customers . . .'

'You also think . . .'

'What do I think?'

'That I killed the butcher?'

'I presume that's impossible, because you were at home at that time . . .'

'No!'

Urbain looked him in the eyes defiantly, and Maigret said, picking up his glass:

'Well, that's more problematic . . .'

3

To tell the truth, Maigret had never particularly liked Urbain, but he would have found it hard to say why. The owner of the Grand Café did his job as café proprietor, smiled or laughed with the customers and came running the minute he was needed for the card game. But perhaps he lacked spontaneity? Often, when he laughed at one of the mechanic's jokes, for instance, he gave the impression that he would rather bite, and sometimes he could be caught darting glances devoid of any pleasantness.

'It's boredom,' Maigret said to himself. 'It's no fun for a man of thirty-five to hang around all day in the sawdust of a provincial café . . .'

And now this same Urbain, after showing vague signs of rebellion and possibly defiance, was giving free rein to his emotion, forgetting all human dignity, in Maigret's dining room where his face crumpled and he suddenly broke down in tears.

'It's the first time I've ever cried in front of a man,' he mumbled in a last attempt to compose himself. 'But the situation is just too ridiculous! If this goes on, I think I'll end up blowing my brains out . . .'

He was in one of those states when, faced with too

great an injustice of fate, a person feels like stamping their feet.

'Why was it that, when you finished the game last night, I had a fit of jealousy? Oh! I know Angèle had promised me not to see "him" again. From next week, she wouldn't even be going to Orléans once a week, as a result of my pleading with her. Even so, yesterday, after spending an hour close to the butcher, thinking that he had . . . Have you yourself never been jealous?'

Maigret merely shook his head with the sanctimonious indifference of a confessor.

'I couldn't stand it any more . . . I went out through the back, as I sometimes do, and, for a quarter of an hour, I stood there in the dark, leaning on the parapet of the bridge . . .'

'Are you certain that no one saw you?'

'Even if someone did see me, it was so dark they couldn't have recognized me . . . Earlier, when the chief inspector from Orléans questioned me, I realized that he suspected all the café regulars, but me more than any of the others . . . Am I going to have to tell him everything? And will my wife have to find out, which means that my home life, which is already not much fun, will become hell? That's what I have come to ask you . . .

'I can't live without Angèle any longer, do you understand? I couldn't say how this love began . . . At first, I think it was simply curiosity . . . Then it became an obsession, to the point where it hurts me when customers look at her or brush past her . . . My wife means nothing to me, these days . . . I'd rather leave her than lose Angèle . . . But I swear, inspector, I didn't kill the butcher . . . !

'What should I do? How can I prove it? What should I say when I'm questioned and am unable to provide an alibi! Who will believe me when I say that I spent those minutes fuming, leaning on the parapet of a bridge?

'I didn't kill him, that's the truth! And my situation is even worse because I would have been capable of doing it, but not like that, from behind, on the road . . .

'Tell me: do you believe me?'

Maigret felt his gaze burning with fever and anxiety on him, and he looked away.

'Please say, do you believe me?'

'I can't answer you . . .'

'So you don't believe me, and you know me! What will those who don't know me think . . . ?'

'Please calm down.'

'That's easy to say!' sneered Urbain.

'There is no suggestion that anyone will bother you . . . Detective Chief Inspector Gabrielli came to see me earlier and he spoke to me briefly about you . . . Any suspicions they may have against one or the other of you are so vague that I believe ultimately the case may well remain unsolved . . .'

He had spoken softly, still without looking at Urbain, and that was so out of character for Maigret that Urbain, frowning, tried in vain to understand what this attitude concealed.

'You think they won't find the murderer?'

'I have no idea . . .'

'Thank you . . . ! I took you for a friend, an ally, if you prefer . . . I was wrong, earlier, to bare my soul in front of you . . . I'm sorry . . . ! You're going to think I have no shame . . .'

'I assure you I don't!' Maigret repeated emphatically.

Why didn't anyone understand that he *couldn't* say anything?

'Go home . . . Try to calm down . . . Stop getting so worked up . . . If you're questioned, answer as you see fit . . . As far as I'm concerned, I have forgotten everything you told me . . .'

But he knew that a man never forgives another for having witnessed him humiliating himself, especially for nothing! Urbain, who had gradually regained his composure, tried to smile, or rather to smirk.

'You must have started to believe that love really does make people mad,' he joked in a phony voice.

'I've seen more tragic cases!' replied Maigret. 'Do you really not want anything to drink?'

'No, thank you . . . ! As you said earlier, there must be a lot of people at my place . . . It's my job to serve drinks, isn't it . . . ? And to make up a fourth when there's a player short . . . Goodbye, inspector!'

He was barely out of sight when Madame Maigret, forgetting her usual tactfulness, said:

'He looked as if he'd been crying . . .'

And, since her husband didn't answer, now she became angry.

'Have you sworn never to open your mouth again? And are you going to sit there all day fretting? You know, I'm beginning to wonder what's behind all this.'

Maigret smiled and said sardonically:

'Actually, you're right. Perhaps I'm the one who killed the poor butcher!'

'Don't be stupid. I'm not talking about the murder, I mean that girl's visit . . .'

'No, please! No jealousy . . .'

'Why not?'

'Because this isn't the time . . . Now look! Things are already sad enough as it is . . . !'

'What's sad?'

'This whole little tragedy . . . Because it's such a little tragedy! So petty! So laughable even, when you think about it! Would you ever imagine that an Angèle could drive two sensible men crazy . . . ?'

'She's the type . . .'

'The poor, sickly looking type of girl . . . ! Undernourished, big eyes with dark rings under them and a pasty complexion that's never seen the sunlight . . .'

'That means nothing.'

'You're right! That means nothing! As we can see from the fact that, for two men, this Angèle embodied the feminine ideal and became their main reason for living . . . I knew that, in some cases, there can be a sort of bewitchment . . . In rural villages, with the solitude, the heat, the doldrums, you see young, good-looking, strong and loyal men fall madly in love with a singer in some dive and fight over her . . .

'It must be because they have nothing to compare her to . . .

'But here . . . ! In a decent town in the heart of the Loire, a few kilometres from Orléans . . . !'

His wife glanced at him, surprised to hear him be so loquacious, which was rare. She didn't dare interrupt him for fear he would stop abruptly.

'And yet . . .' he went on. 'Look! Can you tell me why, every night for more than a year, I'd leave this house at five to five, and why, shortly afterwards, I'd push open the door of the Grand Café, and why, for almost two hours, I'd lay down little coloured cards, with great seriousness, as if my life depended on it?'

'It's not because of her?'

'Don't be silly . . . ! I knew you wouldn't understand . . . I was talking to you about bewitchment . . . Well, that's another form of it . . . A compulsion, if you prefer, a need you create for yourself when you have nothing better to do . . .'

This was the first time he had ventured an allusion to his retirement, but it was not the first time Madame Maigret had thought about it.

'You go there once, twice . . . Then, one fine day, you feel disconcerted if for some reason the game doesn't take place . . . You get used to certain faces, certain jokes . . . You have "your" chair, "your" deck of cards . . .'

He was talking not to her, but to himself. Since that morning, since the previous day, this had been brewing inside him, and it was a relief to give free rein to his disgust.

'That's what it leads to . . . ! So why wouldn't other men, in the same circumstances, not grow fond of a girl and end up seeing her as the centre of their lives?

'I recall people's reactions to crimes of passion, when I

was still at the Police Judiciaire. I'd show them a photograph of a woman, and they would nearly always protest:

'"She's not even attractive! How could someone kill for her?"

'The heroines of crimes of passion are never beautiful! It's a more subtle poison. When Urbain saw one of us inadvertently looking at the girl, he suffered as much as if he had cancer . . . The idea that the butcher . . .

'Are you beginning to understand?'

'Did he kill him?' Madame Maigret had the misfortune to ask in her innocence.

'You too, you're going to keep harping on about that? Is that all that interests you people? Blood! Mystery! Murder! Murder! Murder . . . ! But, for heaven's sake, don't you see there are other things in life?

'I'm trying to explain a tragedy that is painful in other ways, and you're asking me who killed . . .

'Can't you make an effort and imagine that section of street near the bridge, the Grand Café with, in the summer, its terrace and its bay trees in green barrels; opposite, the red shutters of the butcher's shop . . .

'On one side, the butcher's wife, who's in the shop all day long and, every now and then, comes to the doorway to call her kid who's playing in the street . . .

'On the other side, another woman, sad and sickly, and a child, and a man who only thinks of one thing: Angèle!

'This Angèle who isn't beautiful, who probably has no personality and whose little body is devoid of any charm! All the same, the butcher and his neighbour go round in circles, like merry-go-round horses, obsessed with a single idea, both consumed with jealousy, watching each other, glaring daggers at each other and blind to all else . . .

'Now do you understand?'

And Madame Maigret replied:

'I've understood that men are stupid . . . Is that what you wanted to explain to me . . . ? Only, now, what's going to happen? Will he be arrested?'

Then Maigret, in a fit of anger, went up to his room and slammed the door, and, for no reason, turned the key in the lock.

He did not reappear until dinner time, and he was in no better a mood. But he asked cautiously:

'Did anyone come?'

'No!'

'Oh!'

'Are you expecting someone?'

'Me . . . ? No . . . ! What an idea . . . !'

He had done his utmost in a few hours to deter people from appealing to him, but he was still disappointed to see that he had succeeded.

'Are you going out, after dinner?'

'Why would I go out?'

'I don't know . . . I was just wondering . . .'

He didn't go out. The next morning, he went off fishing early, taking a snack with him, and did not come home until four o'clock in the afternoon, with a large pike and perch whitebait.

'The funeral is tomorrow morning . . .' his wife announced. 'Shall I go with you?'

'Why not?'

'The newspaper seems to be suggesting it was a prowler . . . There's not a word about that Angèle . . .'

'So?'

'Nothing . . . I thought—'

'You mustn't think . . .'

He didn't go out any more than he had the previous day. The next day, wearing his black suit and accompanied by Madame Maigret, he attended the butcher's funeral and went all the way to the cemetery. Twice his colleague Gabrielli attempted to engage him in conversation, but each time he pretended to be preoccupied.

Urbain was there, together with Citroën. Angèle, too, was at the church, huddled in a shadowy corner.

'Aren't you going back to the café with them?'

There was a pale sun. Men could be seen entering the Grand Café for an aperitif and to carry on talking about the event.

Maigret preferred to be at home and, for a week, he did nothing but fish obsessively; then he decided to renovate his boat, pulled it ashore on to the grassy bank, and worked on it for several more days, permanently splattered with tar and green paint.

'You know they appear to be dropping the investigation?'

'Why should I care?'

'I thought . . .'

As always happens, once the boat was spruce, he no longer felt like fishing and, since the weather was very mild and the first lilac blossoms were perfuming the bottom of the garden, he spent his time there reading the Duke of Otranto's *Memoirs*.

'Why don't you go and play cards again in the evenings? You used to enjoy it . . .'

He didn't reply. But the simple mention of cards put him in a bad mood.

One day, his wife told him:

'The butcher's shop is up for sale . . . His widow got a hundred thousand francs from the insurance and she's going to live with her sister in Orléans . . .'

No reaction, other than grumpiness still, and it took weeks and weeks for Maigret to get back to more or less his old self.

One day when he'd been out for a walk and came home at around eight in the evening, Madame Maigret commented:

'You're back very late . . .'

'I played backgammon . . .' he admitted.

'At the Grand Café?'

'No, at the Commerce . . . With the new butcher . . .'

'Why have you never wanted to tell me what happened?'

'Because!'

'And now? Can I still not know the truth?'

'No!'

That summer, they decided to visit Savoie, of which they saw very little because Madame Maigret was not a good walker.

4

It was three years later, at around the same time of year, because the lilacs were beginning to bloom. Maigret, in clogs, was planting out tender green lettuces when his wife opened the letterbox and unfolded a death announcement.

'Goodness! She died after all . . .' she said.

'Who?'

'The woman from the Grand Café . . . Madame Urbain . . . The dairy woman told me that for the past three months the only thing she could swallow was milk . . . You'll have to go and drop off your condolence card . . .'

Maigret went there that evening and stayed for a few moments in the chapel of rest, where Angèle was blowing her nose in a corner.

Two days later, the funeral took place and the Maigrets came back from the cemetery arm in arm, on a glorious day that left no room for dark thoughts.

'This reminds me of one of the worst moments of my life . . .' he began suddenly, for no apparent reason.

This time, Madame Maigret had the tact to keep quiet and carry on walking, because they had left the road to make their way home along the bank of the Loire.

'I don't know whether you remember the butcher . . . I knew everything, from the very start, and even, I could say, from the moment I was told the news. But what I knew, I couldn't tell anyone . . . It was a matter of honesty, honesty towards a dead man . . .'

Without thinking, Madame Maigret had picked a daisy, which she held in her hand like in the painting by an artist whose name Maigret had forgotten. They walked slowly, pushing their way through the tall vegetation on their path, and thistles clung to Maigret's trousers.

'What struck me was the butcher's insistence on telling us that he had a lot of money in his pocket . . . Like most provincial shopkeepers, he'd stayed faithful to the wallet . . . He always had a huge one bursting with money, little notes and grubby papers in his trouser pocket, and I remember his movements when he took it out, the apron he had to lift up . . .

'But that evening, he began by conspicuously taking out his wallet and opening it . . . so that we could see it was full . . . But, surprisingly, I had the impression that, although there was a one-thousand-franc note on the top of the wad, underneath, there was only ordinary paper . . .

'That visit to the notary too . . .

'When I was told he'd been murdered, I said to myself: "It's too strange a coincidence . . ."

'Because I've never seen people killed just when they were expecting it . . .

'When I arrived at his place, I checked that, although the money had gone, the wallet had been put back in the dead man's pocket . . .'

'So he wasn't murdered?' asked Madame Maigret, shocked.

'Not at all! And the poor man wasn't even clever enough to disguise his suicide properly. It was amateurish. If they'd sent anyone other than Gabrielli to lead the official investigation, they would soon have realized. But Gabrielli, who is a charming young man, is better at Russian billiards than at detective work . . .'

She smiled and they walked on a little.

'That's why I had to keep quiet . . . That's why I didn't want to hear all those people's secrets . . . But they came to confide in me anyway, whining or begging . . .'

'I still don't understand why the butcher did that . . .'

'Because he was a poor fool, capable of the best and the worst . . . He was crazy about that girl and had entreated her to run away with him and, had she agreed, he'd have dumped his wife and son there and then with no regrets . . . He wouldn't even have spared them a thought . . .

'In any case, he'd already begun to ruin them financially, firstly by not taking care of his affairs any more or by managing them badly, and then by giving Angèle gifts she didn't know what to do with, because she couldn't let Urbain see them . . .

'When she told the butcher she didn't want to see him any more, he decided to kill himself . . . And being unhappy made him more sensitive to the unhappiness of others . . .

'I'm certain that it was at that moment he thought of his wife and son . . . He realized that they would be left in financial difficulties . . . If he was going to die, it may as well serve some purpose . . .

'And that's why he took out an insurance, that's why there could be no question of suicide, that's why the fool was so insistent about going to see the notary and so obligingly showed us his wallet . . .'

'That had never occurred to me . . .' said Madame Maigret. 'I always wondered why you allowed the culprit to go free . . .'

'Others must have asked themselves the same thing, especially since Urbain, by the greatest of coincidences, had no alibi. When he came to tell me that, weeping with anxiety, I thought I was going to have to tell him the truth to prevent him from going to prison . . .

'What can I say? It pained me to see the poor wretch die for nothing . . . Since I'm no longer a member of the police, and I'm not in the pay of the insurance companies . . .'

He stopped, creasing up his eyes in the sunlight, and gazed at the scenery, its charm enhanced by the murmuring waters of the Loire.

'Anyhow, I'm glad it's in the past,' he sighed. 'It was an unpleasant business . . .'

'And you didn't say a word to anyone?'

'Not to anyone!'

'Not even to Urbain?'

'Not even!'

'Or to Angèle?'

He couldn't repress a smile.

'Jealous?'

'Oh! no . . . But now I see what men are like . . . So this bewitchment you told me about once can happen quite simply, out of habit, because a girl serves you an aperitif at the same time every day . . . ?'

He continued to smile, relieved to have been able to tell his story to someone. Especially because now it was over!

The butcher's widow, in Orléans, had remarried. Her new husband worked for the water authority, and the boy called him his uncle.

Once the mourning period was up, there was no doubt that Urbain would wed Angèle.

Today, the café was closed, with a notice edged in black on the shutter.

Madame Urbain was left alone in the cemetery and people made their way back into town, shaking off the last whiffs of death that clung, with the smell of incense, to their shoulders.

'Would you be capable of that?' asked Madame Maigret abruptly, as they were about to turn into the alleyway that led from the river to the wall of their garden.

'Capable of what?'

'I don't know . . . of anything . . . like them . . .'

'You see why one should never tell women anything!' he teased, cupping his hands to light his pipe with a match.

And he asked mechanically:

'What's for lunch? I'm starving!'

The Man on the Streets

The four men were wedged together in the taxi. Paris was freezing. At half past seven in the morning, the city was ghostly pale and the wind was chasing the ice powder along the ground.

The thinnest of the four, on a fold-down seat, had a cigarette stuck to his lower lip and handcuffs on his wrists. The burliest, with a heavy jaw, wearing a thick overcoat and bowler hat, watched the railings of the Bois de Boulogne flashing past.

'Do you want me to make a noisy scene?' the handcuffed man offered amiably. 'With contortions, foaming at the mouth, swearing and the works . . . ?'

Maigret grunted, removed the cigarette from the man's lips and opened the door, because they had arrived at Porte de Bagatelle:

'Don't try to be too clever!'

The avenues of the Bois de Boulogne were empty, white as cut stone and as hard. A dozen or so people were pacing up and down on the corner of a bridle path, and a photographer wanted to snap the approaching group. But Li'l Louis raised his arm to cover his face, as he'd been advised to do.

Maigret, looking surly, turned his head, bearlike, studying everything, the new apartment buildings on Boulevard Richard-Wallace, their shutters still closed, a few labourers on bicycles coming from Puteaux, a lit-up tram, two concierges walking towards them, their hands purple with cold.

'Is that it?' he asked.

The previous day, he had allowed the following announcement to be published in the newspaper:

THE BAGATELLE MURDER

For once, it did not take the police long to shed light on a case that appeared to present overwhelming difficulties. We know that on Monday morning, in an avenue of the Bois de Boulogne, around a hundred metres from Porte de Bagatelle, a park ranger discovered a body which it was possible to identify on the spot.

The dead man was Ernest Borms, a well-known Viennese doctor who has lived in Neuilly for several years. Borms was in evening dress. He must have been attacked during the course of Sunday night as he was walking back to his apartment on Boulevard Richard-Wallace.

He had been shot through the heart at point-blank range with a bullet from a small-calibre revolver.

Borms, who was still young, good-looking and extremely elegant, was a socialite.

Barely forty-eight hours after this murder, the Police Judiciaire has just made an arrest. Tomorrow morning, between seven and eight o'clock, there will be a reconstruction of the crime at the scene.

Afterwards, at Quai des Orfèvres, this case was referred to as possibly the most emblematic of Maigret's method of working. But when his colleagues spoke of it in front of him, he had a strange way of gazing elsewhere and grunting.

Right! Everything was in place. Hardly any onlookers, as anticipated. It was no coincidence that he had chosen this early hour. And among the ten or fifteen people hanging around were some police officers trying their best to keep a low profile. One of them, Torrence, who loved disguises, was dressed as a milkman, which made his chief shrug.

So long as Li'l Louis didn't go too far . . . ! An old customer, arrested the previous day for pickpocketing in the Métro . . .

'You're going to help us out tomorrow morning, and we'll make sure the judge doesn't come down too heavily on you . . .'

They'd hauled him out of the cells.

'Let's go!' said Maigret. 'When you heard footsteps, you were hidden over here, is that right?'

'Like you say, inspector, sir . . . I was starving, you see . . . Skint! . . . So I said to myself that a fellow walking home in a dinner-jacket must have a bulging wallet . . . "Your money or your life!" I hissed in his earhole . . . And I swear to you it's not my fault if the gun went off . . . I reckon it's the cold that made my finger slip on the trigger . . .'

Eleven o'clock in the morning. Maigret was pacing up and down in his office at Quai des Orfèvres, smoking his pipe, constantly fiddling with the telephone.

'Hello! Is that you, chief? . . . Lucas, here . . . I followed the old man who seemed to take an interest in the reconstruction . . . Nothing doing on that front . . . He's a madman who goes for his little stroll in the Bois every morning . . .'

'Fine! You can come back . . .'

Eleven fifteen.

'Hello, chief? . . . Torrence! . . . I tailed the young man you indicated out of the corner of your eye . . . He sits every detective recruitment exam . . . He's a sales assistant in a store on the Champs-Élysées . . . Shall I come back?'

At five to twelve, finally, a call from Janvier.

'I'll be quick, chief, or I'm afraid the bird will fly . . . I'm watching him in the little mirror in the phone booth door . . . I'm at the Nain Jaune, Boulevard Rochechouart . . . Yes . . . He's spotted me . . . He's got a guilty conscience . . . As he walked over the bridge, he threw something into the Seine . . . Ten times he tried to lose me . . . Shall I wait for you?'

That was the start of a hunt through a completely oblivious Paris that was to last five days and five nights, among hurried pedestrians, from bar to bar, café to café, a lone man, on the one hand, and, on the other, Maigret and his officers working in shifts, and, by the end, becoming as exhausted as the man they were stalking.

Maigret alighted from the taxi opposite the Nain Jaune at aperitif time, and found Janvier leaning on the bar. He didn't bother to try to keep a low profile. On the contrary!

'Which one is it?'

Janvier jerked his chin in the direction of a man sitting at a pedestal table in a corner. The man watched them with clear blue-grey eyes that marked him out as a foreigner. A Scandinavian, a Slav? More likely a Slav. He was wearing a grey overcoat, a well-cut suit and a fedora.

Mid-thirties, as far as Maigret could tell. He was pale and close-shaven.

'What will you have, chief? A hot Picon?'

'Yes to a hot Picon . . . What's he drinking?'

'Brandy . . . The fifth since this morning . . . Sorry if I'm slurring, but I've had to follow him into all the bars . . . He's tough, you know . . . Look at him . . . This has gone on all day . . . He wouldn't lower his eyes for all the world . . .'

It was true and it was strange. His expression could not be called disdain, or defiance. The man was simply staring at them. If he was anxious, he wasn't showing it. His gaze was full of sadness more than anything, a calm, pensive sadness.

'At Bagatelle, when he noticed you were watching him, he immediately walked away and I followed on his heels. He hadn't gone a hundred metres before he turned around. Then, instead of leaving the woods as he seemed to have the intention of doing, he ran off with great strides down the first avenue he came across. He turned around again. He recognized me. He sat down on a bench, despite the cold, and I stopped . . . Several times, I had the feeling he wanted to speak to me, but eventually he walked off with a shrug . . .

'At Porte Dauphine, I almost lost him, because he jumped into a taxi, and it was a stroke of luck that I found one almost straight away. He got out at Place de l'Opéra, and dived into the Métro . . . With me on his heels, he changed lines five times, and he started to realize that he wouldn't shake me off that easily . . .

'We came back above ground at Place Clichy. Since then, we've been going from bar to bar . . . I waited for a suitable place with a telephone booth from where I could watch him. When he saw me making a call, he gave an unpleasant little snicker . . . My word, I could have sworn then that he was waiting for you . . .'

'Call Headquarters . . . Tell Lucas and Torrence to be ready to join me the minute I phone . . . And also a photographer from Criminal Records, with a very small camera . . .'

'Waiter!' called the stranger. 'How much do I owe you?'

'Three fifty . . .'

'I bet he's a Pole . . .' Maigret muttered to Janvier. 'We're off . . .'

They didn't go far. At Place Blanche, they entered a little restaurant just behind the man, and sat at the table next to his. It was an Italian restaurant, and they ate pasta.

At three o'clock, Lucas came to relieve Janvier, who was with Maigret in a brasserie opposite the Gare du Nord.

'The photographer?' asked Maigret.

'He's waiting outside to snap him as he comes out . . .'

And, when the Pole left the establishment, having read the newspapers, a police officer scooted towards him. At less than a metre away, he clicked the shutter. The man quickly raised his hand to his face, but it was already too late, and then, to show he understood, he shot Maigret a look full of reproach.

'You, my man,' said Maigret to himself, 'you have good

reasons not to lead us to your home. You may have a lot of patience, but I have just as much as you . . .'

That evening, a few snowflakes fluttered down on to the streets while the stranger walked, his hands in his pockets, waiting until it was time to go to bed.

'Shall I take over from you for the night, chief?' offered Lucas.

'No! I'd rather you concentrated on the photograph. Check the records, first. Then go and pay a visit to the foreign communities. This fellow is familiar with Paris. He isn't newly arrived. There must be people who know him . . .'

'Supposing we published his picture in the papers?'

Maigret gazed at his subordinate scornfully. Did Lucas, who'd been working with him for so many years, not understand? Did the police have a single clue? Nothing! No eyewitness! A man is murdered in the middle of the night in the Bois de Boulogne. No weapon has been found. No fingerprints. Doctor Borms lived alone, and his only servant doesn't know where he went the previous evening.

'Do as I say! Go on . . .'

At midnight, finally, the man decided to walk into a hotel. Maigret went in behind him. It was a second- or even third-rate establishment.

'I need a room . . .'

'Would you fill out the form?'

He did so, hesitantly, his fingers numb with cold.

He looked Maigret up and down, as if to say:

'If you think this bothers me . . . ! I can write anything I like . . .'

And he wrote the first name that came into his head, Nicolas Slaatkovitch, residing in Cracow, arrived in Paris the previous day.

It was clearly untrue. Maigret telephoned the Police Judiciaire. They combed through the files of the lodging houses, the registers of foreigners, and alerted the border posts. No Nicolas Slaatkovitch.

'A room for you too?' asked the owner, frowning, because he'd smelled a police officer.

'No thank you. I'll spend the night on the staircase.'

It was safer. He sat down on a stair, outside the door of room 7. Twice, the door opened. The man scanned the dark hallway, spotted Maigret's form, and eventually went to bed. By morning, Maigret had grown a stubble and his cheeks felt rough. He hadn't been able to change his underwear. He didn't even have a comb, and his hair was tousled.

Lucas had just arrived.

'Shall I take over, chief?'

Maigret couldn't bring himself to leave his stranger. He watched him pay for his room. He saw him blanch. And he guessed.

A little later, in a bar where they stood side by side, so to speak, drinking a café-crème and eating croissants, the man counted up his worldly wealth without trying to hide the fact. A one-hundred-franc note, two twenty-franc coins, one ten and some small change. His lips curled in a bitter grimace.

Well! He wouldn't get far with that. When he'd arrived at the Bois de Boulogne, he must have just left home because he was clean-shaven, without a speck of dust, without a single crease in his clothes. Presumably he'd been planning to return a little later. He hadn't even checked whether he had money in his pocket.

Maigret guessed that what he had thrown into the Seine had been ID documents, and perhaps calling cards.

He wanted to prevent his address from being discovered, at all costs.

And the vagrant's wanderings began anew: loitering outside shops, in front of pavement sellers, going into bars every so often if only to sit down, especially since it was cold outside, reading newspapers in the brasseries.

One hundred and fifty francs! No more restaurant at lunchtime. The man made do with hard-boiled eggs, which he ate standing at a bar, washed down with half a pint of beer, while Maigret wolfed down sandwiches.

The man dithered for a long time outside a cinema. His hand jingled the coins in his pocket. Better hold out . . . He walked . . . And walked . . .

Come to think of it! A detail struck Maigret. This exhausting ramble always took them through the same neighbourhoods; from the church of La Trinité to Place Clichy . . . From Place Clichy to Barbès-Rochechouart, via Rue Caulaincourt . . . From Barbès to the Gare du Nord and Rue La Fayette . . .

Was the man afraid of being recognized elsewhere? Doubtless he'd chosen the neighbourhoods the furthest from his home or his hotel, the districts he didn't usually frequent . . .

Did he haunt Montparnasse, as many foreigners did? The area around the Panthéon?

His clothes suggested that his circumstances were average. They were comfortable, simple and well cut. Liberal profession, probably. Look! He wore a ring! So he was married!

Maigret had to resign himself to handing over to Torrence. He stopped by his apartment. Madame Maigret was annoyed because her sister had come from Orléans and she'd cooked an elaborate dinner and, after shaving and changing his clothes, her husband was already off again, saying he didn't know when he'd be back.

He raced over to Quai des Orfèvres.

'Did Lucas leave anything for me?'

Yes! There was a note. Lucas had shown the photo in various Polish and Russian circles. The man was unknown to them. No luck among the political groups either. In desperation, he had a large number of prints made of the photograph. Police officers were going from door to door in every Paris district, speaking to the concierges and showing the photo to bar owners and café waiters.

'Hello! Inspector Maigret? I'm an usherette at the Ciné-Actualités newsreel theatre, Boulevard de Strasbourg... There's a gentleman... Monsieur Torrence... He told me to call you to tell you that he's here, but he daren't leave the auditorium...'

Not so daft, this man! He'd reckoned that this was the best warm place to spend a good few hours cheaply... Two francs to get in... and you're allowed to sit through several screenings!

★

A strange intimacy had developed between the pursuer and the pursued, between the man, whose beard was growing, whose clothes were becoming crumpled, and Maigret, who wasn't letting him out of sight for an instant. There was even a comical detail. They had both caught colds. They both had a red nose. When they took their handkerchiefs out of their pockets, they were almost synchronized, and at one point, the man couldn't suppress a vague smile on seeing Maigret have a sneezing fit at the same time as him.

A seedy hotel on Boulevard de la Chapelle, after five consecutive newsreel screenings. Same name in the register.

And Maigret, once again, sat himself on a stair. But, since it was a call house, he was disturbed every ten minutes by couples who stared at him with curiosity, and the women felt ill at ease.

When the man reached the end of his tether or was worn out, would he decide to go home? In a brasserie, where he sat for quite a while and had taken off his grey overcoat, Maigret had no hesitation in grabbing the garment and looking inside the collar. The overcoat came from the Old England, on Boulevard des Italiens. It was off the peg, and the establishment must have sold dozens of similar overcoats. A piece of information, all the same. It was from the previous winter. So the stranger had been in Paris for at least a year. And during that year, he must have lived somewhere . . .

Maigret began drinking hot toddies, to knock out his cold. The man only parted with his money in dribs and drabs. He drank coffees, not even laced with alcohol. He ate croissants and hard-boiled eggs.

News from Headquarters was always the same: nothing to report! No one recognized the photo of the Pole. No one had been reported missing.

As for the dead man, no new developments there either. He owned a large practice. He made a very good living, was not involved in politics, went out a lot and, since he treated nervous diseases, saw mainly women patients.

One experiment that Maigret hadn't yet had the opportunity to see through to the end was finding out how long it took for a well-bred, well-groomed, well-dressed man to lose his outer veneer when he was left to roam the streets.

Four days! Now he knew. First of all, the beard. The first morning, the man looked like a lawyer, a doctor, an architect or an industrialist, and you could picture him leaving a plush apartment. A four-day beard transformed him to the extent that if his photo had been published in the papers in connection with the Bois de Boulogne case, people would have said:

'You can see he looks like a murderer!'

His eyes were red-rimmed from the freezing temperatures and lack of sleep, and his cheeks were flushed from his cold. His shoes, now scuffed, had lost their shape. His overcoat was worn and his trousers were sagging at the knees.

Even his gait . . . He no longer walked the same way . . . He skulked . . . He lowered his eyes when passers-by stared at him ... Another detail: he turned away when he walked past a restaurant where customers could be seen sitting at tables in front of copious dishes ...

'Down to your last twenty francs, poor fellow!' calculated Maigret. 'And then what?'

Lucas, Torrence and Janvier relieved him from time to time, but he handed over to them as little as possible. He popped into Quai des Orfèvres and saw the superintendent.

'You ought to get some rest, Maigret ...'

A grouchy, prickly Maigret, as if torn between contradictory feelings.

'Is it my duty to find the murderer, yes or no?'

'Of course ...'

'I'll be on my way, then!' he sighed with a note of bitterness in his voice. 'I wonder where we're going to sleep tonight ...'

Only twenty francs left! Not even that much! When he joined Torrence, the latter informed him that the man had eaten three hard-boiled eggs and drunk two coffees laced with alcohol in a bar on the corner of Rue Montmartre.

'Eight francs fifty ... Leaving eleven francs fifty ...'

He admired him. Instead of hiding, he walked abreast of him, sometimes beside him, and he had to make an effort not to speak to him.

'Come on, my friend ... Don't you think it's time to sit down and have something to eat? Somewhere there's a warm home waiting for you, a bed, slippers, a razor ... Hmm? And a good meal ...'

But no! The man prowled under the arc lights of Les

Halles like those who have nowhere to go, among the mounds of cabbages and carrots, stepping aside at the whistle of the train or the rumble of the market gardeners' drays.

'Can't afford a room any more!'

The Meteorological Office recorded a temperature of minus eight that night. The man treated himself to hot sausages which a vendor cooked in the howling wind. He was going to reek of garlic and grease all night!

At one point, he tried to slip inside a market hall and stretch out in a corner. A police officer, to whom Maigret hadn't had time to give instructions, sent him packing. Now, he was limping. The banks of the Seine. The Pont des Arts. Let's hope he doesn't impulsively throw himself into the river! Maigret didn't feel brave enough to jump after him into the dark water that was beginning to freeze over.

He followed the towpath. Vagrants groaned. Under the bridges, the best spots were taken.

In a side street near Place Maubert, old men were visible through the windows of a strange café, sleeping with their heads on the tables. For twenty sous, with a glass of red wine thrown in! The man glanced at him in the darkness. He gave a fatalistic shrug and pushed the door. As it opened and closed behind him, Maigret received a nauseating whiff in his face. He preferred to stay outdoors. He called an officer and stationed him on the pavement to stand guard while he went and telephoned Lucas, who was on duty that night.

'We've been looking for you for an hour, chief. We've found something! Thanks to a concierge . . . The guy is called Stephan Strevzki, architect, age thirty-four, born in

Warsaw, living in France for three years . . . He works for an interior designer in Faubourg Saint-Honoré . . . Married to a Hungarian woman, a gorgeous girl by the name of Dora . . . Lives in an apartment that costs twelve thousand francs a month in rent, Rue de la Pompe in Passy . . . No politics . . . The concierge has never seen the victim . . . Stephan left on Monday morning, earlier than usual . . . She was surprised not to see him come back home, but she wasn't worried when she noticed that—'

'What time is it?'

'Half past three . . . I'm on my own here . . . I had some beer brought up, but it's very cold . . .'

'Listen, Lucas . . . you're going to . . . Yes! I know! Too late for the morning editions . . . but in the evening ones . . . Understood?'

That morning there was a faint odour of poverty clinging to the man's clothes. His eyes were more sunken. The look he shot Maigret, in the pale dawn, contained the most pathetic of rebukes.

Had he not been brought, little by little, but at a vertiginous speed all the same, down to the bottom rung of the ladder? He turned up his overcoat collar. He didn't leave the neighbourhood. He dived into a café that had just opened, a wry grimace on his face, and downed four glasses of spirits in quick succession, as if to chase away the horrible aftertaste that the night had left in his throat and in his chest.

Too bad! Now, he had nothing left at all! All he could do was pace the streets that were slippery with black ice.

He must be aching. His left leg was limping. Every so often, he would stop and look about him in despair.

From the moment the man stopped going into cafés where there was a telephone, Maigret could not ask anyone to relieve him. The riverbank again! And that automatic gesture of the man rummaging through the second-hand books, turning the pages, sometimes checking the origins of an engraving or a print! An icy wind swept over the Seine. Ahead of the moving barges, the spangled water made a rattling sound as tiny chunks of ice clinked together.

From a distance, Maigret could see the Police Judiciaire, his office window. His sister-in-law had gone back to Orléans. Let's hope that Lucas . . .

He didn't know yet that this gruesome investigation would become legendary, and that generations of police officers would repeat the story to newcomers. The stupid thing was that it was a ridiculous detail that upset him the most: the man had a pimple on his forehead, a pimple which, looking at it closely, must be a boil, and was turning from red to purple!

Let's hope that Lucas . . .

At midday, the man, who definitely knew his Paris well, was walking towards the soup kitchen at the far end of Boulevard Saint-Germain. He joined the queue of down-and-outs. An old man said something to him, but he pretended not to understand. Then another, with a pock-marked face, spoke to him in Russian.

Maigret arrived at the pavement opposite, hesitated, was forced to eat sandwiches in a café, and half turned his back so that through the window the man wouldn't see him eating.

The poor wretches shuffled slowly forward, going in fours or sixes into the room where they were given bowls of hot soup. The queue grew longer. From time to time, there was pushing and shoving at the back, and some protested.

One o'clock... The kid was approaching from the far end of the street... He was running, his body thrust forward...

'*L'Intran*... Get *L'Intran* here...'

He too was trying to get there before the others. He could identify from a distance the passers-by who would buy a paper. He didn't bother with the line of down-and-outs.

'Get—'

Humbly, the man raised his hand and said:

'Pssssttt!'

The others stared at him. So he still had a little change to buy a newspaper?

Maigret hailed the vendor in turn, and unfolded the paper, relieved to find what he was looking for on the front page: the photo of a woman – young, beautiful, smiling.

A WORRYING DISAPPEARANCE

We were informed, four days ago, of the disappearance of a young Polish woman, Madame Dora Strevzki, who has not returned to her home at 17, Rue de la Pompe in Passy.

> *A worrying detail: the missing woman's husband, Stephan Strevzki, disappeared from his home himself the day before, in other words on Monday, and the concierge, who called the police, states . . .*

The man only had another five or six metres to go in the queue that was carrying him along, before he received his bowl of steaming soup. At that moment, he stepped out of the line, crossed the street, almost getting hit by a bus, and reached the opposite pavement where Maigret happened to be just in front of him.

'I'm at your disposal!' he simply said. 'Take me away . . . I'll answer all your questions . . .'

They were all in the corridor of the Police Judiciaire – Lucas, Janvier, Torrence, and others who had not worked on the case but who knew about it. As Maigret walked past, Lucas made a sign that meant:

'This is it!'

A door opened and closed. Beer and sandwiches on the table.

'Have something to eat first . . .'

Embarrassment. Mouthfuls he couldn't swallow. Then, at last, the man:

'As long as she's gone and is safe somewhere . . .'

Maigret felt the urge to riddle the stove.

'When I read about the murder in the papers . . . For a long time I'd suspected Dora of being unfaithful to me with that man . . . I also realized she wasn't his only mistress . . . I knew Dora, she's impulsive . . . Do you understand? If he'd wanted to dump her, I knew that she was capable of . . . And she still had a pearl-handled pistol in her handbag . . . When the papers reported the arrest of the murderer and the reconstruction of the crime, I wanted to see . . .'

Maigret wished he could say, like the English police:

'I warn you that anything you say may be given in evidence against you . . .'

The man had not taken off his overcoat. He was still wearing his hat.

'Now that she's safe . . . Because I presume . . .'

He looked about him anxiously. A suspicion went through his mind.

'She must have realized, when I didn't return home . . . I knew it would end like this, that Borms wasn't a man for her, that she would never agree to be a plaything for him and then she'd come back to me . . . She went out alone, on the Sunday evening, as she had been doing recently . . . She must have killed him when . . .'

Maigret blew his nose. He blew his nose long and hard. A ray of that particular winter sunshine that accompanies icy spells slanted through the window. The pimple – the boil – shone on the forehead of the man, whom he was unable to call anything except the man.

'Your wife killed him, yes . . . When it dawned on her that he'd been making a fool of her . . . And you, you knew she'd killed him . . . and you didn't want . . .'

Suddenly, he went over to the Pole.

'I apologize, my friend,' he growled, as if speaking to an old pal. 'My job was to find out the truth, wasn't it? My duty was to . . .'

He opened the door.

'Show in Madame Dora Strevzki . . . Lucas, you continue, I . . .'

And for two days, no one saw any more of him at the Police Judiciaire. The chief telephoned him at home.

'I say, Maigret . . . You know she confessed everything and that . . . By the way, how's your cold? . . . I've heard . . .'

'It's nothing, chief! I'm absolutely fine . . . In twenty-four hours . . . What about him?'

'What . . . ? Who . . . ?'

'Him!'

'Ah! I understand . . . He hired the best lawyer in Paris . . . He's hoping . . . you know, crimes of passion . . .'

Maigret went back to bed and knocked himself out with hot toddies and aspirin. When, later, anyone tried to talk to him about the investigation . . .

'What investigation . . . ?' he'd grunt in such a way as to deter questions.

And the man came to see him once or twice a week to keep him abreast of the lawyer's hopes.

It wasn't exactly an acquittal, but one year's suspended sentence.

And this was the man who taught Maigret to play chess.

Candle Auction

Maigret pushed away his plate and the table, stood up, grunted, shuddered and without thinking lifted up the cover of the stove.

'Let's get to work, my friends! We'll go to bed early!'

And the others, sitting around the inn's large table, turned their resigned faces towards him. Frédéric Michaux, the owner, whose beard had grown bushy in three days, was the first to get to his feet, and he went over to the bar.

'What would you—'

'No! Enough!' shouted Maigret. 'Enough white wine, then calvados, then more white wine and . . .'

They had all reached the point of exhaustion where their eyelids were tingling and their entire bodies ached. Julia, Frédéric's wife, took a plate with the cold remains of a dish of kidney beans into the kitchen. Thérèse, the little servant girl, wiped her eyes, not because she was crying, but because she had a head cold.

'When do we start again?' she asked. 'When I've cleared the table?'

'It's eight o'clock. So we'll start again at eight o'clock tonight.'

'So I'll bring the mat and the cards . . .'

It was warm inside the inn, too warm even, but outside in the night the wind was blowing gusts of sleet.

'Sit down where you were, old Nicolas . . . And you, Monsieur Groux, you hadn't arrived yet . . .' instructed Maigret.

The owner interrupted. 'It was when I heard Groux's footsteps outside that I said to Thérèse: "Put the cards on the table . . ."'

'Do I have to pretend to come in again?' complained Groux, a farmer six foot tall and built like a tank.

They looked like actors rehearsing a scene for the twentieth time, their minds empty, their movements limp, their eyes expressionless. Maigret himself, who was playing the part of the director, sometimes had difficulty convincing himself that all this was real. Even the place where he was! What a crazy idea to spend three days at an inn in the middle of nowhere, miles from the nearest village, in the heart of the Vendée marshlands!

The place was called Pont-du-Grau, and there was an actual bridge, a long wooden bridge over a sort of murky canal that was swollen by the tide twice a day. But the sea wasn't visible. There was nothing but wetlands crisscrossed by countless rivulets, and, on the distant horizon, flat-roofed farmhouses known in those parts as *cabanes*.

Why this roadside inn? For duck and lapwing hunters? There was a red petrol pump and the gable end was covered in a giant blue advertisement for a brand of chocolate.

Across the bridge, a traditional farmstead, a real rabbit hutch, the home of old Nicolas, the eel fisherman. Three hundred metres away stood a large farm with long, single-storey buildings: Groux's property.

. . . on 15 January . . . at 13:00 precisely . . . in the locality of La Mulatière . . . public auction of a farmstead . . . thirty hectares of wetland . . . equipment and livestock . . . agricultural machinery . . . furniture, crockery . . .

Cash buyer only.

That had been the start of it all. For years, life at the inn had been the same every evening. Old Nicolas would arrive, always half-drunk, and would go and have a little glass of wine at the bar before sitting down with his bottle. Then Groux would come over from his farm. Thérèse would spread out a red mat on the table and bring the cards and the tokens. They'd have to wait for the customs officer to make up the fourth, or, when he wasn't there, it was Julia who took his place.

On 14 January, the eve of the sale, there were two extra guests at the inn, farmers who had come a long way for the auction. One of them was Borchain, from the Angoulême area, and the other Canut, from Saint-Jean-d'Angély.

'Hold on!' said Maigret as the owner was about to shuffle the cards. 'Borchain went to bed before eight o'clock, immediately after he'd eaten. Who showed him to his room?'

'I did!' replied Frédéric.

'Had he been drinking?'

'Not much. Certainly a little. He asked me who the glum-looking fellow was, and I told him it was Groux, whose property was being sold . . . Then he asked me how Groux had managed to lose money with such good wetlands, and I—'

'That's enough!' Groux objected.

The giant was gloomy. He didn't want to admit that he'd never taken proper care of his land or his livestock and blamed the heavens for his loss.

'Right! At that point, who had seen his wallet?'

'Everyone. He'd taken it out of his pocket when he was eating, to show a photo of his wife . . . So we saw it was stuffed with bills . . . Even if we hadn't seen it, we'd have known, because he'd come with the intention of buying, and the sale had been advertised as cash only . . .'

'So Canut, you also had more than a hundred thousand francs on you?'

'A hundred and fifty thousand . . . I didn't want to go any higher . . .'

On arrival at the scene, Maigret, who was head of the Nantes Flying Squad at the time, examined Frédéric Michaux from head to toe and frowned. Michaux, who was in his mid-forties, hardly looked like a country innkeeper with his boxer's pullover and broken nose.

'Tell me . . . Don't you have the feeling we've met somewhere before?'

'No point wasting time . . . You're right, inspector . . . But I've gone straight now . . .'

Pimping in the Ternes neighbourhood, assault and battery, illegal betting, slot machines . . . In short, Frédéric Michaux, innkeeper at Pont-du-Grau, in the most far-flung part of the Vendée, was better known to the police as Fred the Boxer.

'You'll probably recognize Julia too . . . You banged us

both up ten years ago... But you'll see how conventional she's become...'

It was true. Julia, fatter, bloated, ill-kempt and greasy-haired, dragging her slippered feet from the kitchen to the restaurant and from the restaurant to the kitchen, was nothing like the Julia of Place des Ternes and, most surprisingly, her cooking was first class.

'We brought Thérèse with us... She's a ward of the state...'

Eighteen, a long, slender body, a pointed nose, an odd mouth and a brazen stare.

'Do we have to play for real?' asked the customs officer, whose name was Gentil.

'Play as you did last time. You, Canut, why didn't you go to bed?'

'I was watching the game...' mumbled the farmer.

'That's to say he was chasing after me all the while,' added Thérèse, aggressively, 'and making me promise that I'd go up to his room later...'

Maigret noticed that Fred was glaring daggers at the man and that Julia was looking at Fred.

Right... They were in place... And, that evening too, it was raining... Borchain's room was on the ground floor, at the end of the passage... There were three doors leading off that same passage: one into the kitchen, another that opened on to the stairs down to the cellar and a third with the number 100 on it.

Maigret sighed and wiped his forehead wearily. He'd been there for three days and he reeked of the smell of the place; the atmosphere clung to his skin, making him feel nauseous.

And yet, what else could he do but what he was doing? On the 14th, just before midnight, while the card game was still being played half-heartedly, Fred had sniffed the air a few times. He'd called Julia, who was in the kitchen.

'Is there something burning in the oven?'

He had got up and opened the door to the passage.

'Christ, it stinks of smoke here!'

Groux had followed him, and Thérèse. It was coming from the guest's room. He knocked. Then he opened the door, which had no lock.

It was the mattress that was slowly burning, a wool mattress, which gave off an acrid odour of grease. On this mattress lay Borchain, in shirt and long johns, his skull smashed.

They had a telephone. At 1 a.m. Maigret was informed. At 4 a.m. he arrived in the midst of a downpour, his nose red, his hands frozen.

Borchain's wallet had disappeared, the window was closed. No one could have got in from the outside because Michaux had a not-very-friendly German shepherd dog.

Impossible to arrest them all. But all of them were suspects, apart from Canut, the only one not to have left the main room all evening.

'Go on, my friends! I'm listening to you . . . I'm watching you . . . Do exactly as you did on the 14th, at this time . . .'

The sale had been postponed. Throughout the day of the 15th, there had been a stream of people outside the inn and Maigret had ordered the doors to be locked.

Now it was the 16th. Maigret had not left this room, so to speak, except to go and sleep for a few hours. Nor had any of the others. They were sick of seeing one another all day long, of hearing the same questions again and again, of replicating the same gestures.

Julia did the cooking. They forgot the rest of the world. It took an effort to remember that there were people living elsewhere, in the towns, who were not endlessly repeating:

'Let's see . . . I'd just cut hearts . . . Groux laid down his cards saying:

' "There's no point playing . . . Not one card comes my way . . . My usual luck . . . !"

'He stood up . . .'

'Stand up, Groux!' ordered Maigret. 'Just as you did the other day . . .'

The giant gave a shrug.

'How many times are you going to send me to the privy?' he grumbled. 'Ask Frédéric . . . Ask Nicolas . . . Don't I usually go at least twice . . . ? Don't I . . . ? What do you think I do with the four or five bottles of white wine I've drunk during the day?'

He spat and headed for the door, walked down the passage and punched open the door marked 100.

'There! Do I have to stay in it, at this hour?'

'For as long as is necessary, yes . . . and the rest of you, what did you do while he was out of the room?'

The customs officer laughed nervously at Groux's anger, and there was something cracked in his laughter. He was the least robust of all. His nerves were on edge.

'I told Gentil and Nicolas that it would turn ugly,' said Fred.

'That what would turn ugly?'

'Groux and the farm . . . He'd always believed that the sale wouldn't go ahead, that he'd manage to borrow some money . . . When the bailiff came to put up the poster, he threatened him with his gun . . . At his age, when you've always been a landowner, it's not easy to go and work for someone else . . .'

Groux had come back without saying a word and was glaring at them.

'Now what?' he shouted. 'Are we done, or not? Am I the one who killed the man and set the mattress on fire? Then say so right away and throw me into jail . . . At this stage . . .'

'Where were you, Julia? I have the feeling you weren't in your usual place . . .'

'I was peeling vegetables in the kitchen . . . We were expecting a lot of people at lunchtime, because of the sale . . . I'd ordered two legs of lamb, and we'd only just finished one . . .'

'Thérèse?'

'I went up to my room . . .'

'At what point?'

'Shortly after Monsieur Groux came back . . .'

'Well! We're going to go up there together . . . The rest of you, continue . . . Did you return to your game?'

'Not straight away . . . Groux didn't want to . . . We talked . . . I went to get a packet of Gauloises from the bar.'

'Come on, Thérèse . . .'

The room where Borchain had died was very

strategically located. The staircase was only two metres away. And so Thérèse could have . . .

A narrow room, an iron bedstead, underwear and clothes on a chair.

'What did you want up here?'

'To write . . .'

'Write what?'

'That we probably wouldn't be alone for a moment the next day . . .'

She looked him in the eyes, defiantly.

'You know very well what I'm talking about . . . I could tell from your looks and your questions . . . The wife's suspicious . . . She's always on our backs . . . I begged Fred to take me away, and we'd decided to run off in the spring.'

'Why in the spring?'

'I don't know . . . It was Fred's decision . . . We were supposed to go to Panama, where he used to live, and we planned to open a café . . .'

'How long did you stay in your room?'

'Not long . . . I heard the wife coming up. She asked me what I was doing . . . I said *nothing* . . . She hates me and I hate her . . . I could swear she'd got wind of our plans . . .'

And Thérèse held Maigret's gaze. She was one of those girls who know what they want and are single-minded.

'Don't you think Julia would rather see Fred in prison than have him run off with you?'

'She's capable of it!'

'What was she going to do in her room?'

'Take off her belt . . . She needs a rubber belt to support her bits . . .'

Thérèse's pointed teeth made him think of a small rodent, and she had the same instinctive cruelty. As she spoke of the woman who had preceded her in Fred's affections, her lips curled.

'At night, especially when she's eaten too much – she stuffs herself so full, it's disgusting! – her belt stifles her and she goes upstairs to take it off . . .'

'How long did she stay up there?'

'Ten minutes, maybe . . . When she came back down, I helped her peel the vegetables . . . The others were still playing cards . . .'

'Was the door between the kitchen and the restaurant open?'

'It's always open . . .'

Maigret looked at her again, and lumbered down the stairs, which creaked. He could hear the dog in the courtyard, straining on its chain.

When the cellar door was opened, just behind it was a heap of coal, and it was from this heap that the murder weapon had been taken: a heavy coal hammer.

No fingerprints. The killer must have grabbed the tool with a cloth. Elsewhere in the inn, including on the doorknob of the bedroom, were numerous smudged fingerprints, those of everyone who had been there on the evening of the 14th.

As for the wallet, ten of Maigret's men had hunted for it, in the most unlikely places, men who were used to these kinds of searches, and on the previous day they'd called in the maintenance company to empty the septic tank.

Poor Borchain had come from his rural home to buy

Groux's smallholding. Until then, he had only been a farmer. He wanted to become a landowner. He was married and had three daughters. He'd eaten at one of the tables. He'd chatted with Canut, who was also a potential buyer. He'd shown him the photograph of his wife.

Drowsy from a copious meal washed down with a great deal of wine, he had gone off to bed, with that gait farmers have when it is time to go to sleep. Most likely he slid the wallet under his pillow.

In the restaurant, four men played belote, like every evening, drinking white wine: Fred, Groux, old Nicolas who turned crimson when he was drunk, and the customs officer Gentil, who would have done better to go on his rounds.

Behind them, straddling a chair, Canut with one eye on the cards and the other on Thérèse, hoping that this night away from home would allow him to have a little fling.

In the kitchen, two women: Julia and the orphan girl, over a vegetable bucket.

One of these characters, at a given moment, had gone into the passage on some pretext or another and opened the cellar door to seize the coal hammer, and then entered Borchain's room.

No one had heard anything. That person couldn't have been missing for long, because their absence hadn't seemed unusual.

And yet, the murderer still had to put the wallet somewhere safe!

Because, since they'd set fire to the mattress, the alarm would soon be raised. The police would be called. Everyone would be searched!

'And you don't even have any decent beer!' grumbled Maigret, going back into the main room.

A glass of cool draught beer with a good head! Whereas the inn only had bottles of a nasty local ale!

'What about this game?'

Fred looked at the time on the promotional clock with a sky-blue earthenware surround. He was used to the police. He was tired, like the others, but less frazzled.

'Twenty to ten . . . not yet . . . We were still talking . . . Was it you, Nicolas, who asked for more wine?'

'Possibly . . .'

'I shouted to Thérèse: "Go and draw some wine . . ." Then I got up and went down to the cellar myself.'

'Why?'

He shrugged.

'Too bad, isn't it? Let her hear, after all! When all this is over, life won't be the same as before . . . I'd heard Thérèse go up to her room . . . I thought she'd probably written me a note . . . It would be in the lock of the cellar door . . . Do you hear, Julia? I can't do anything about it, old thing! You've created enough scenes to make me pay for our rare moments of pleasure . . .'

Canut turned red. Nicolas quietly sniggered into his reddish-brown beard. Monsieur Gentil looked away, because he too had made advances to Thérèse.

'Was there a note?'

'Yes . . . I read it down below, while the wine was running into the bottle. Thérèse simply said that we probably wouldn't have a moment alone together the next day . . .'

Strange thing, one sensed in Fred a sincere passion and

even an unexpected degree of emotion. In the kitchen, Thérèse abruptly got to her feet, and she went over to the card players' table.

'It's over, isn't it?' she said, her lips trembling. 'I'd rather we all got arrested and sent to prison. We'll see . . . But beating about the bush like this, pretending . . . pretending . . .'

She burst into tears and went and flung her arms against the wall, burying her head in them.

'So you stayed in the cellar for several minutes,' Maigret continued, unperturbed.

'Three or four minutes, yes . . .'

'What did you do with the note?'

'I burned it in the flame of the candle . . .'

'Are you afraid of Julia?'

Fred resented Maigret for using that word.

'You don't understand, do you? Even though you arrested us ten years ago! You don't understand that when two people have been through certain things together . . . Well! As you wish . . . ! Don't worry, my poor Julia . . .'

And a calm voice came from the kitchen:

'I'm not worried . . .'

The motive, the famous motive that all the books on criminology mention? Every one of them had a motive! Especially Groux, who was at the end of his tether, who would be sold the following day, thrown out of his home, unable to take even his furniture or his livestock, and who had no option but to hire himself out as a farmhand!

He knew the place, the door to the cellar, the coal heap, the hammer . . .

What about Nicolas? An old alcoholic, granted. He lived in poverty. But he had a daughter in Niort. She had found a job as a maid, and everything she earned went towards paying for her child's keep. Could he not have . . .

Not to mention, as Fred had said earlier, that it was he who came every week to split the wood and smash the coal!

But, at around ten o'clock, Nicolas had gone to the toilet, lurching like a drunkard. Gentil had commented:

'Let's hope he doesn't get the wrong door!'

There are such coincidences! Why had Gentil said that as he automatically shuffled the cards?

And why might not Gentil have thought of murder when, a few moments later, he'd followed in old Nicolas' tracks?

Admittedly, he was a customs officer, but everyone knew he didn't take his job seriously, that he did his rounds in the cafés and it was always possible to come to an arrangement with him.

'Well, inspector . . .' began Fred.

'Excuse me . . . It's five past ten . . . What were you doing the other night at that time?'

Then Thérèse, who was sniffing, came and sat behind her boss, brushing his back with her shoulder.

'Were you there?'

'Yes . . . I'd finished the vegetables . . . I picked up the jumper I'm knitting but I didn't do any work on it . . . Julia was still in the kitchen, but we couldn't see her.'

'What were you trying to say, Fred?'

'An idea occurred to me . . . There's a detail that proves that it wasn't one of us who killed the man . . . Because . . .

Think about it . . . No! That's not what I mean . . . If I were to kill someone in my own inn, would I set the place on fire . . . ? Why . . . ? To attract attention . . . ?'

Maigret had just filled a fresh pipe and was lighting it slowly.

'Give me a small calvados, Thérèse! As for you, Fred, why wouldn't you have started a fire?'

'Well, because . . .'

He was taken aback.

'If it hadn't been for the fire breaking out, we wouldn't have been worried about the fellow . . . the others would have gone home . . . and . . .'

Maigret smiled, his lips strangely stretched around the stem of his pipe.

'A pity that you have proved exactly the opposite of what you wanted to prove, Fred . . . The fire breaking out is the only real clue, and it struck me from the moment I arrived . . . Supposing you kill the man, as you say . . . Everyone knows he's staying here . . . so there's no way you can dispose of the body . . . The next morning, you would have to open his door and raise the alarm . . . What time did he ask to be woken up, by the way?'

'At six o'clock . . . He wanted to visit the farm and the land before the sale . . .'

'If then the body was discovered at six o'clock, the only people here were you, Julia and Thérèse, because I'm not counting Monsieur Canut, whom no one would have suspected . . . No one would have imagined either that the murder could have been committed during the card game . . .'

Fred listened attentively to Maigret's reasoning, and it seemed to Maigret that he had grown paler. He even tore up a playing card, without thinking, dropping the shreds on to the floor.

'Careful, if you try to play later, you won't be able to find the ace of spades . . . As I was saying . . . Ah! yes . . . How could the murder be discovered before Groux, Nicolas and Monsieur Gentil left, so that suspicion would fall on them . . . ? No reason to go into the room . . . Oh yes there was! Just one . . . the fire . . .'

This time, Fred sat bolt upright, his fists clenched, a hard glint in his eyes, and he yelled:

'To hell with it!'

Everyone was silent. They had just received a shock. Up till then, they had been so weary that they'd stopped believing there was a murderer. They no longer realized that he was there, at the inn, that they were speaking to him, eating at the same table, and perhaps playing cards with him and clinking glasses.

Fred paced up and down with great strides while Maigret sat hunched, his eyes narrowed. Was he going to succeed at last? For three days he'd kept them on tenterhooks, minute by minute, making them repeat ten times the same gestures and the same words with the hope, of course, that a forgotten detail would suddenly surface, but above all with the aim of breaking their nerve, of pushing the killer to the limit.

He spoke in a calm voice, the syllables punctuated by little puffs on his pipe.

'The entire question is to know whether he had a secure

enough hiding place close at hand guaranteeing that the wallet couldn't be found . . .'

Everyone had been searched. One after the other, on the infamous night, they had been stripped stark naked. The coal heap in the cellar had been turned over. The walls and barrels had been probed. All the same, a fat wallet containing more than a hundred thousand-franc notes . . .

'You're making me seasick, pacing up and down like that, Fred . . .'

'But dammit, don't you understand that . . .'

'That what?'

'That I didn't kill him! That I'm not crazy enough to do that! That I've got a bad enough criminal record to—'

'It was in the spring that you intended to run off with Thérèse to South America and buy a café, wasn't it?'

Fred turned towards the kitchen door and asked between clenched teeth:

'So?'

'With what money?'

His eyes bored into Maigret's.

'Is that what you're leading up to? You're on the wrong track, inspector. Money, I'll have on 15 May. I had a conventional idea when I was earning a nice living organizing boxing matches. I took out an insurance policy for one hundred thousand francs, which matures when I'm fifty.

'And I'll be fifty on 15 May . . . Yes, Thérèse, I've notched up a few more years than I normally admit to . . .'

'Did Julia know about this insurance?'

'It's none of women's business!'

'So, Julia, you were unaware that Fred was going to receive a hundred thousand francs?'

'I knew.'

'What?' cried Fred, startled.

'I also knew that he wanted to run off with that hussy...'

'And you would have let them leave?'

Julia kept absolutely still, gazing at her lover, and there was a strange serenity about her.

'You haven't answered my question!' Maigret pressed her.

She turned to look at him. Her lips moved. Perhaps she was going to say something important? But she shrugged.

'Can a person know what a man will do?'

Fred wasn't listening. It was as if suddenly he had something else on his mind. He was frowning, thinking, and Maigret had the impression that their thoughts were following the same path.

'Tell me, Fred!'

'What?'

It was as if he'd been woken from a dream.

'About that insurance policy... that policy that Julia saw without your knowing... I'd like to have a look at it too...'

What an unpredictable route the truth was taking to emerge! Maigret believed he'd thought of everything. In her room, Thérèse had talked to him of leaving, therefore money... Fred admitted to the existence of the insurance policy...

But... It was so simple, so idiotic that he nearly burst out laughing: the place had been searched twice but no insurance policy, or identity documents or military service record had been found.

'At your disposal, inspector,' sighed Fred calmly. 'And you'll also find out how much I have in savings . . .'

He headed towards the kitchen.

'You can come in . . . When you live in a godforsaken place like this . . . Not to mention that I've got some papers that my pals from the past would like to get their paws on . . .'

Surprised, Thérèse followed him. Groux's heavy tread could be heard, and Canut also rose.

'Don't think it's particularly smart . . . It so happens that I was a boilermaker in my youth . . .'

To the right of the stove was a huge galvanized-iron refuse bucket. Fred turned it upside down right in the middle of the room and flipped out a false bottom. He was the first to look. Slowly his expression turned to a frown. Slowly he looked up and opened his mouth . . .

There was a fat wallet, grey from wear, held together with a band of red rubber tubing from a tyre, among various papers.

'*Well, Julia?*' Maigret asked softly.

Then he had the impression of glimpsing, behind the mistress of the house's plump features, something of the Julia she had been. She gazed at them all. Her upper lip curled in scorn. It was possible she was stifling a sob. But it did not burst out. In a flat voice, she said:

'And now what? I'm done for . . .'

The most extraordinary thing was that Thérèse was the one who suddenly started screaming, like a dog baying for blood, whereas the woman who had killed asked:

'I suppose you're going to take me away right now, since you have the car . . . Can I bring my belongings . . . ?'

He let her pack her bag. He was sad: the reaction, after a long spell of nervous tension.

When had Julia discovered Fred's hiding place? On finding the insurance policy, which he'd never told her about, had it dawned on her that he would run off with Thérèse when the money came through?

An opportunity arose: even more money than Fred would receive! And she was the one who would give it to him, in a few days' time, in a few weeks, once the case had been closed!

'Listen, Fred . . . I knew about everything . . . You wanted to go off with her, didn't you? . . . You thought I was no longer good for anything . . . Open your hiding place . . . It's me, the old woman as you call me, who . . .'

Maigret, just in case, watched her as she came and went into the bedroom where there was just a big mahogany bed with a photo of Fred as a boxer above it.

'I have to put my belt back on,' she said. 'I'd rather you didn't look. It's not a pretty sight.'

It wasn't until they were in the car that she broke down, while Maigret stared fixedly at the raindrops on the windows. What were the others at the inn doing now? And who would Groux's farm be sold to when the third auction candle burned itself out?

Death Threats

I

'Hello! Is that you, Maigret? Would you step into my office for a moment?'

This month of June was glorious, and the windows overlooking the Seine were flung wide open. Maigret took advantage of the summons to put a stop to the confidences of a rather dubious individual who'd contrived for his trafficking to be disregarded in exchange for coming into the Police Judiciaire each week to inform on his fellow dealers in Montmartre.

A few moments later, Maigret pushed open the padded door to the office of the superintendent and, there too, the tall windows were open, letting the light stream into a room where all the Paris crimes were brought to a conclusion.

'Come in, Maigret. Let me introduce . . .'

Maigret hadn't yet seen the customer about to be presented to him, but already he knew that this was a somewhat unusual case, simply from the look on the face of the chief, with whom he'd already worked on the Bonnot affair, as he spoke these opening words:

'Monsieur Émile Grosbois, the famous rag and scrap metal merchant of Rue du Chemin-Vert . . .'

A surreptitious wink that meant:

'You're going to enjoy this!'

Maigret, turning around, found himself facing a short, dowdy, pallid man who was trying to smile as he held out a freckled hand. His hair was probably ginger, but was so sparse that it was hard to tell its colour.

'Very honoured, detective chief inspector . . . I've heard a lot about you . . .'

'Do sit down.'

The chief handed Maigret a scrap of paper with a message made from words and letters cut out from newspapers.

'Read this.'

Poor Monsieur Grosbois did not suspect what this exchange meant for the two men, who had known each other for such a long time and had seen so many human specimens:

'Watch out! The fellow looks like a crafty old devil . . .'

Out loud, of course, the chief said exactly the opposite:

'Monsieur Grosbois, who is very well connected, comes warmly recommended by a municipal councillor whom he met earlier today . . .'

'I thought—' began Grosbois.

'Don't apologize! You've done the right thing! When you're well in with influential people, it is natural to use them.'

Meanwhile, Maigret read:

Old scoundrel,

This time you're done for. Whether you go to Coudray or not, even if you are protected by a regiment of gendarmes, you will die before 6 p.m. on Sunday.

And everyone will be glad to be rid of you.

No signature, of course. Maigret had difficulty suppressing a smile as he observed his ashen customer.

'Naturally,' the chief was saying, 'Monsieur Grosbois has no idea who would send him such a letter. He's not aware of having any enemies . . .'

'We've always been considered reputable in our business dealings!' stated Monsieur Grosbois.

And the chief went on:

'I pointed out to him that the Police Judiciaire's remit does not extend beyond Paris. If the murder is committed in the city, it is our concern. But if someone is killed in Coudray . . . Monsieur Grosbois was so insistent that I agreed to take on the case, since happily no murder has yet been committed. What do you think, Maigret? Would you mind very much spending the weekend in Coudray?'

'Is it by the Seine, just beyond Corbeil? If that is so, I know the area a little. A few years ago, I had to investigate a murder at the Citanguette lock . . .'

'So you'll take charge of the case?'

'If you wish, chief!'

'Monsieur Grosbois tells me he doesn't have a car. He himself doesn't drive and chauffeurs have become intolerably demanding . . .'

Knowing wink.

'The entire family takes the train on Saturdays after lunch. The railway line goes through the property itself and the station is only fifty metres from the house . . .'

Monsieur Grosbois rose, shook the two men's hands and left, mumbling his thanks.

As soon as the door had closed behind him, the head of

the Police Judiciaire and Maigret were finally able to relax their expressions.

'Did you notice, chief?'

'It depends what you mean.'

'That the small pocket on his jacket is on the right! In other words, his suit has been reversed.'

'I simply noted that he had rubber heels on so as not to wear out the ones on his shoes . . .'

'How many millions?'

'The Grosbois are said to have amassed around thirty.'

'What do you think of this threat?'

'I don't think anything yet. In any case, I've warned our man that if this is a wheeze to claim life insurance, we'll inform the company and it won't work. You remember that Russian who disguised his suicide as a murder so that his daughter could get a large insurance payout?'

'I was the one who led the investigation,' said Maigret modestly.

'I was forgetting . . . May I . . . ?'

The chief picked up the telephone, which had just rung.

'Hello, yes . . . Monsieur Grosbois? . . . Oscar Grosbois? . . . Monsieur Émile's brother? . . . Very well! . . . I'll pass you over to Detective Chief Inspector Maigret, who has kindly agreed to take charge of this case . . .'

Maigret took the receiver.

'Hello! . . . Forgive me for bothering you, inspector, but I know my brother came to see you this morning. I absolutely must speak to you. Yes! . . . Could I drop in to your office? . . . You would rather come and see me? . . . In that case, would you come between eleven o'clock and midday, because that's the time my brother goes to the bank? . . . Thank you, inspector . . . Ring the bell by the little door to the right of the wall . . . Thank you . . . Thank you . . .'

Maigret hung up and sighed:

'And I'd promised my wife that we'd go to the country!'

It was 11.15 when Maigret arrived at Rue du Chemin-Vert, a narrow, lively street in the Bastille neighbourhood, lined mainly with workshops and warehouses.

He found Grosbois & Paget easily: a high wall, a metal gate, a vast courtyard full of carts and enclosed by sheds. He noticed immediately that there were bars on all the windows, which suggested there was a general atmosphere of suspicion, and he rang the bell of the little door as instructed.

A maid in her forties, of dubious cleanliness, came and opened the door, and said, before he could open his mouth:

'Go up to the first floor. Monsieur Oscar's expecting you.'

Monsieur Oscar was already at the top of the stairs. He resembled his brother so closely that Maigret thought for a moment that he was dealing with the same man.

'I'm sorry to have put you to all this trouble, inspector . . . I would gladly have met you in your office . . .'

Maigret couldn't admit to him that he had preferred to visit in person because he quite fancied having a little sniff around the establishment.

'Come in! These old buildings aren't very practical but, when you're born in one . . .'

Maigret could have replied that, just because a person is born in a place, that's no reason to leave it untouched for decades. Already, the fake marble staircase walls had turned a drab ditchwater brown. The carpet was colourless and had faded to its greyish threads.

'This is a household of bachelors, which explains the mess . . .'

But no! There was no mess! It was dirty and neglected! The dusty furniture looked as if it had been bought from the flea market and a profusion of hideous vases and ghastly knick-knacks made the place look like the back room of a junk shop in a poor neighbourhood.

'Have a seat, inspector. Can I offer you a cigar?'

He held out a little silk-paper sachet which proved he had been anticipating this visit and had gone out and bought half a dozen cigars from the tobacconist's on the corner. Oscar Grosbois' gesture was serious, almost solemn. Could offering a cigar be a way of redeeming a guilty conscience?

'Thank you, I prefer my pipe.'

'I don't smoke. Nor does my brother. I wonder what on earth he's told you. He's such a strange fellow!'

Maigret didn't dare move because one leg of the chair in which he was sitting threatened to give way under his weight.

'You have of course noticed how alike we are. We're twins, as you thought . . . We have an older sister, Françoise, who lives on the second floor with her children—'

'So your sister is married?'

'She was married to a certain Paget. Hence the

company name you saw: Grosbois & Paget. Her husband died ten years ago, and she was left a widow with a son and a daughter.'

'In other words, the entire family still lives in the building?'

'Not only here, but also in our country house in Coudray. We enjoy family life, the simple life . . .'

Maigret felt like saying:

'You must be joking!'

'Times are tough. We don't know what the world is coming to. But that's not what this is about. My brother must have shown you a letter he claims to have received yesterday morning?'

At the word 'claims' Maigret pricked up his ears.

'He showed it to us too, and he seemed quite distraught. I calmed him down as best I could, because it's obviously a prank . . .'

'You, my friend,' Maigret said to himself, 'you're dying to know what I think!'

He refrained from responding and looked at Monsieur Oscar with an indescribable candour.

'I assume that people planning to commit a murder aren't in the habit of warning their victims . . .'

'It has been known to happen.'

'In some cases, perhaps . . . ? But who could hold a grudge against us . . . ? We've never harmed anyone . . . We don't owe a cent . . . We . . .'

That ineffable stare of Maigret's embarrassed him and he found it hard to resume his train of thought.

'A little aperitif, inspector? We don't drink either . . .

No! We've led a healthy, simple life . . . Never any alcohol or tobacco . . . ! But that doesn't mean we don't have the necessary for our guests . . .'

'Do you entertain a lot?'

'Never! I was saying . . . Oh yes . . . I was saying that my poor brother recently—'

'He's unmarried, like you, isn't he?'

'We're two old bachelors . . . Fifty-three years old, both of us . . . and I would never have thought that one day my brother would become . . . How can I put it?'

If Maigret had been asked to describe the man in front of him, he would have said that he had the face of a rat with anxious, prying eyes that darted everywhere.

'I don't want you to take what I'm saying literally . . . Émile isn't mad . . . most of the time he has his wits about him . . . However, there are moments when . . .'

Still Maigret deliberately held back from coming to his rescue, and Oscar was floundering.

'. . . when he's not as he has always been . . . You understand . . . ! He gets annoyed . . . He has whims. I'll go a lot further, but please keep this to yourself . . . I wouldn't be surprised if Émile had written the letter he showed you himself . . . It's what's known as persecution mania, if I'm not mistaken . . . That's what I wanted you to know . . . I have too much respect for the police to let you get involved in a case that probably has no grounds whatsoever and you would probably have reprimanded me for saying nothing . . .'

Just then, Maigret strained to listen, because from the

floor above, the sounds of an argument could be heard through the thin floorboards.

Oscar Grosbois gave a start too, and mumbled:

'It's the children squabbling!'

'Your sister's children? How old are they?'

'Henri is twenty. His sister Éliane is eighteen. At that age, brother and sister are a bit like cat and dog . . .'

Oscar's smile was unattractive, revealing pointed little yellow teeth, rodent's teeth.

'Is your nephew in the rag business?'

'No . . . ! He's studying . . .'

'What is he studying?'

'Business . . . He hasn't quite made up his mind yet . . . His mother has spoiled him a great deal . . .'

The noise from upstairs turned into a real commotion and, if it was an argument between brother and sister, it must have turned into a serious fight. Eventually there was the sound of running feet, shouting, doors slamming and then footsteps on the stairs.

'Don't take any notice . . . These are the little drawbacks of family . . . To get back to my brother, you've been warned . . . Don't attach too much importance to his words, and above all to his fears . . . He works too hard . . . If he would only take a month's holiday somewhere quiet, preferably at a health spa in the mountains, for example, he would no longer appear so . . . Are you sure you don't want a cigar?'

And the poor man, gauche as ever, held out the pack of cigars to Maigret, as if giving to charity:

'Go on! Let yourself be tempted! You can smoke them at home . . .'

'I'm going to spend the weekend at the home of people who have thirty million francs!' Maigret had told his wife.

'At least you won't be bored!'

He'd replied with a mysterious smile:

'You don't think so?'

He had taken the Saturday mid-afternoon train, when the carriages are almost full. His train pass allowed him to travel first class, and he found himself sitting opposite a young woman who shocked the entire compartment.

It was hard to determine her exact age, but she was very young, exhibiting a carefree, youthful exuberance. An elderly lady from Melun, in her corner, took her for a 'woman of ill repute' because of the girl's heavy make-up, figure-hugging dress and the brazen way she looked at the people around her.

As for the conversation . . . !

Because the girl was not alone: she was with a young man, a sporty type, hatless, also dressed in an outlandish fashion.

'What did they do?' he asked.

'When they realized that the Bugatti had broken down and there was no godforsaken village for at least five kilometres, the four of them bedded down as best they could in the car, and spent the night there . . .'

'No kidding?'

'The hilarious thing is that, before, Betty was with Jean and Raymonde with Riri . . . I don't know what happened during the night, but, the next day, it was Betty who was with Riri and Jean with Raymonde...'

The elderly lady, sitting stiffly in her corner, glared at the girl with a severity that should have floored her. But she wasn't floored at all. With a total lack of modesty, she hitched her dress right up to straighten her stockings, saying to her companion:

'Did Yolande get hold of any dough?'

'She wrote to her parents telling them she needed an urgent operation to remove her appendix. They sent her ten thousand francs... But before the holidays she'll have to get a scar...'

'That's not hard!'

The old lady's gaze, now resting on Maigret, seemed to be saying:

'The youth of today!'

And Maigret gave a vague smile, enjoying this afternoon of warm sunshine and the countryside flashing past on either side of the train.

'Coudray-Montceaux!'

He leaped up. The young woman too. The young man, however, stayed on the train, which moved off again at once.

Two men were waiting on the platform of the tiny station, both wearing grey alpaca suits, so alike that they looked as if they were a performing duo.

Maigret went up to them and shook their hands, but saw that they were looking past his shoulders. Eventually Émile Grosbois said:

'What time do you call this?'

'I missed the first train . . .'

'What about your brother?'

'I haven't seen him. I thought he was already here!'

It was the outlandish young woman, who was introduced to him as Éliane Paget, the Grosbois brothers' niece.

'Detective Chief Inspector Maigret, of the Police Judiciaire . . .'

'Oh!'

A rather hard, wary gaze.

'Is mother here?'

'She came with us and Babette.'

'I'm going to get changed,' announced Éliane, removing her hat and clambering over a hedge between the station and a garden.

The house was close by, a huge dark-brick construction dating from the worst pre-war years, with hideous ceramic ornamentations. A lawn gave the illusion of gardens, and was adorned with two ugly statues, while the rest of the grounds were a wilderness.

'Something occurred to me, inspector,' began Émile Grosbois. 'If someone wants to take my life, they would probably come by train. Now, from your window, you'll be able to see all the passengers who alight at Coudray. You've noticed that there aren't many . . .'

An extraordinary, troubling impression! The location was magnificent. The Seine was very wide at this point, flowing lazily between two wooded hills and forming a great loop. The sun was beginning to set, tingeing the sky pink.

A scene that exuded the joys of life!

But Maigret was there in the company of two artful little ginger-haired men who were spying on him and on each other.

Instead of the cheeriness evoked by the words 'country house', the sombre edifice oozed boredom, spitefulness and suspicion.

'Don't go that way, inspector, there are traps . . . Let's take the path . . .'

Nondescript front steps. A dim entrance hall which already gave off a faint odour of damp.

'We'll show you your room . . . The bathroom is at the end of the corridor . . . In summer, there's no hot water, because the bath is connected to the central heating, which we only have on in winter . . .'

Maigret glimpsed the maid who had opened the door to him at Rue du Chemin-Vert and who looked busy. He heard a woman's voice calling from the kitchen:

'Babette . . . ! Where are you, Babette . . . ? I can't find the butter . . . I bet you forgot to buy butter again . . . !'

'This way, Monsieur Maigret!' said Émile Grosbois. 'I must thank you for coming. If you knew how much of a comfort your presence here is to me! I, who have never harmed anyone!'

It was pathetic, grotesque! Meanwhile, Éliane appeared in the corridor in a bathing costume, with the tall, sturdy figure of American girls. In contrast to everything that was mouldering in the house, she radiated life and health.

'Aren't you going for a swim?' she asked Maigret.

'I confess I haven't brought my swimming trunks.'

'My brother will lend you some when he gets here.'
Émile Grosbois sighed:
'My sister has raised her so badly . . . ! You saw how she was dressed . . . She'll stay like this until tomorrow evening, and will barely bother to put on any clothes at mealtimes . . .'

Maigret didn't dare tell him that he was delighted by her and that he'd rather gaze at Éliane's shapely form than the horrible sight of the two brothers.

'This is your room . . . The wallpaper's a bit faded, but the countryside is very damp . . . I imagine you would like to get changed . . . ?'

Not at all! Maigret had only brought a razor, a pair of pyjamas and a toothbrush.

'You'll find me in the billiards room . . .'

To think that down there, just before the bend in the river, healthy, muscular, lively young people had set up camp and were diving exuberantly into the Seine!

People who didn't have thirty million francs!

2

Families are capable of having an outsider live among them for weeks, months even, without revealing anything of the shameful little secrets that are the dirty linen of any household.

The Grosbois too must have promised themselves that they would give Maigret a favourable impression, and the proof was the two brothers' affectionate attitude towards each other when they had come to meet Maigret at the station.

The same was true of their sister Françoise, whose first appearance was all sweetness and light. She was coming out of the kitchen, drying her hands.

'Excuse me,' she said, with a faint smile at the corner of her lips. 'I'm not dressed yet. This old house is so impractical and we only have one maid . . .'

Maigret noted inwardly:

'You, my girl, you're the complaining type! A victim of fate, forever bemoaning your lot and looking for sympathy . . .'

As for the brothers, they would have liked to carry on giving the impression of two peace-loving men without malice. And frankly, at first glance, they almost succeeded, with their mouse-grey suits, straw hats, canvas shoes and that mincing walk of theirs, as if they were pensioners taking the air in the garden.

But in less than an hour, this mask had already dropped. Babette had just served tea on the iron garden table. Émile Grosbois took a sort of snuffbox from his pocket and swallowed a tablet from it. At once, Oscar, unable to contain himself any longer, exclaimed:

'You see, inspector! He's taking a tablet, isn't he? And in an hour's time, it will be a pill! Then, with his meal, drops of something or other, and later, yet another medicine . . .'

He gestured to signal that this underlined his theory that his brother was half mad.

'I take care of myself as I think best!' retorted Émile sharply.

'You mean you're unhinged! You're exhausted, that's certain, and what you need is rest. But from that to believing that you're suffering from all the diseases you find in your medical book and stuffing yourself with medicines . . .'

'Each to his own obsession!'

'Yours is ridiculous!'

'I know people with more dangerous ones!'

And Maigret thought:

'Round one! While waiting for round two, I'd be curious to know what Oscar's obsession is!'

Meanwhile Éliane, in a very skimpy swimming costume, was bathing in the river, where a young man soon swam towards her. Maigret could have sworn it was the young man from the train, who must have alighted at the next station.

Round two! They had barely sat down to eat. The menu was uninspired: vegetable soup, potato omelette, spinach and cheese.

Éliane, who had been sunbathing, still had oil on her skin that was very fragrant, and she'd merely slipped a flimsy robe over her bathing costume.

It was Émile, this time, who attacked:

'Françoise! What have I told you a hundred times?'

The poor woman looked about her anxiously, like someone who is used to being rebuked. She was wondering what was wrong now.

'I understand, mother! Uncle Émile would like me to go and get dressed . . .'

'Decently, yes!' confirmed Émile. 'Anyone walking in here unexpectedly would wonder whether they were in a reputable household . . .'

And Éliane retorted as she stood up:

'They'd be more likely to think they were in a lunatic asylum! As for what there is to eat, I'd rather leave!'

Round three! They ate in silence, and there were two empty chairs at the table: Éliane's and one other. Françoise stared at her plate. After a while, Émile remarked:

'Once again, Henri hasn't shown up yet!'

'He's probably been held up by his business . . .' ventured the mother.

And the uncle sniggered bitterly:

'His business! You dare talk about his business?'

'Émile!'

She indicated Maigret, who was hunched over his plate and eating everything that came within his reach.

'You have a funny way of bringing up your children! It's true that if they take after their father . . .'

'Émile!'

But no. He was determined to have his say. He addressed Maigret:

'I should tell you, Monsieur Maigret, that my sister made an unfortunate marriage: to a man who only wed her for our money and who had affairs. Luckily, he died, otherwise I don't know what would have become of this family!'

Françoise was fighting back her tears. Then everyone gave a start. A car pulled up in front of the garden gate, and drove off again at once. They heard footsteps. A young man came in, thin, pale, his face troubled, and said:

'I missed the train! I'm sorry . . .'

Without noticing Maigret's presence, he sat down at his place, asking in surprise:

'Isn't Éliane here?'

Then he saw the stranger, frowned, and looked at each person in turn, waiting for an explanation.

'Did *she* drive you here?' asked his uncle.

Émile clearly couldn't refrain from showing his ill humour for long. He had just taken drops of some medicine. He drank a little-known mineral water and ate special bread.

'Will you answer me?'

'You'll only yell at me!'

The uncle was indeed yelling.

'First of all, I'd like you to show more respect! Secondly, I am perfectly entitled to worry when I see my nephew, at the age of twenty, incapable of doing any job but playing the gigolo to a bit-part actress . . .'

He turned to Maigret.

'This boy is the lover of a kept woman! Look at him! There are days when he can't stand up and I wonder what will become of him . . .'

'Émile!' begged Françoise, sniffing.

In the meantime, Oscar carried on watching Maigret as if to say:

'Did I lie to you? Isn't my brother half mad?'

As for Henri, he replied:

'I don't ask to come here every weekend . . .'

Maigret said to himself:

'As for you, young man, either I'm very much mistaken or you have a cocaine habit!'

From that moment, unusually for him, he began taking notes in the fat black notebook which he always kept on him.

His notes from that Sunday lunchtime read as follows:

Charming family! They cultivate hatred the way others cultivate traditional values. I wonder if there's a single one of them who doesn't hate all the others, and one person in particular.

Émile Grosbois is an obsessive who acts the domestic tyrant and has a terrible dread of dying and of losing money. Like all tyrants, he is suspicious of those around him, spends his time spying on them and suspecting them of the most evil designs.

Oscar has a vice, or an obsession of his own. His brother alluded to it. But what is it, exactly? He must be as tight-fisted as Émile. The latter, as nearly always happens with twins, has the upper hand and Oscar doesn't dare shake off the yoke.

Françoise is frightened of her brothers. She's the punch-bag for all the others' anger and they blame her for her children's shortcomings.

As for Éliane, rather than confronting the storms and putting up with all the pettiness, she selfishly leads her own life. Last night, I heard a noise coming from her room. I'm convinced that the young man from the train came to visit her. Her uncles must be scared of her because, if she gets married, it is almost certain that she'll demand her share of the fortune.

Henri, on the other hand, is a weak, petulant boy who will quickly go off the rails if he carries on taking drugs. Easy prey for a clever woman who gives him the illusion of the high life.

Had one of them sent the threatening note to Émile Grosbois and was it possible that this threat would actually be carried out?

The previous day, in the office of the head of the Police Judiciaire, the two men hadn't really thought so, scenting rather a tasteless prank, or a strange ruse by Émile Grosbois himself.

Since Maigret had been in the house, he no longer took things so lightly and his initial unease deepened, turning into apprehension.

Because, in the glorious setting on the banks of the Seine where Sunday had brought entire flotillas of canoes and anglers lining the banks, it was hard to imagine a more suffocating atmosphere than that of the Grosbois' country home.

Nothing was clear, clean, sincere! And if the walls oozed damp, if the wallpaper was peeling, if the kitchen was dirtier than the seediest restaurant, the occupants matched the decor.

On this subject too, Maigret had taken notes, because he foresaw that, at a certain moment, the tiniest details would become important.

It was, as it were, the list of clashes.

1. Saturday, at tea time, Oscar criticized Émile for his obsession with medication and Émile alluded to his brother's secret vice.
2. At dinner, first spat between Émile and Éliane.
3. Émile goes for Henri, who answers back.
4. In the kitchen, shortly afterwards, argument between Babette and Françoise. Babette is the one who raises her voice. What is the argument about? Immediately afterwards, Françoise, who is crying, slinks upstairs to bed.
5. Next morning, in the garden, spat between Henri and Éliane. Henri seems to suspect that his sister entertained a young man in her bedroom and he speaks to her angrily. Éliane replies in the same tone. They both stop at the approach of their uncle Émile.
6. Less than a quarter of an hour later, in an upstairs corridor, Émile, furious, lashes out at Françoise.

7. Almost at the same moment, Oscar furtively comes up to me and whispers: 'I warned you! Sooner or later, we'll have to have him locked up. We can't carry on living like this . . .'

The entire family was used to breathing this atmosphere, at least! But Maigret felt gloomier than he had ever felt.

Was it possible then that people who had both money and health could have so little sense as to ruin their lives in this way? What insidious disease was eating away at them? And why didn't one of them suddenly burst out laughing and shout:

'Enough of this stupidity! Let's stop squabbling, spying on one another, hating one another . . . The sun's shining . . . It's Sunday . . . Life is beautiful . . .'

But no! Only Éliane reacted this way in her own fashion, insofar that, without worrying about the others, gloriously immodest in her swimming costume, she ran down to the river where she was soon seen in a canoe in the company of a young man.

Meanwhile, Henri was lying in the long grass near the ditch, and when Maigret came across him, he stared hazily at him.

Maigret decided to sit down beside him and begin a conversation.

'Tell me, young man, I get the impression that your uncles don't exactly make your life easy . . .'

Henri didn't reply at first. He was chewing a wisp of straw and his dilated pupils showed that he had taken drugs.

'But you're about to become an adult in the eyes of the law! Then you'll be able to claim your father's share and . . .'

'What business is it of yours?'

'Perhaps I'm poking my nose into what doesn't concern me, but let me remind you that your uncle Émile begged me to come to this house, which isn't exactly fun and games . . .'

'Tough luck!'

Maigret was familiar with these young people who are tense, aggressive and always quick to attack, but who, deep down, aren't truly bad.

'As you wish,' he grunted, walking off.

There was no routine in the household. In short, they literally did nothing all day.

The two brothers, who were up and dressed in their grey alpaca suits from eight o'clock in the morning, sat for a while in garden chairs; then one of them would wander into the house, probably in search of someone to shout at; then they'd meet up and lazily exchange a few words while Françoise worked in the kitchen with Babette.

They were there as a matter of principle, because they had a country house and it had been decided, once and for all, that the entire family would spend their weekends there.

No matter that they were bored! The main thing was being there, around Uncle Émile, who took a perverse pleasure in spying on his little world and picking on the tiniest infringements of the rules he had laid down.

*

'What can Oscar's vice be?' Maigret had wondered a hundred times, studying the man with rodent features. 'He doesn't smoke and he doesn't drink. Stingy as he is, as both brothers are, I'd be surprised if he was a womanizer . . .'

The reply was provided before lunch. Maigret had to do as everyone else did, that is, to come and go between the garden and the house.

At around ten o'clock, Babette went upstairs to tidy the bedrooms. Maigret, walking down the first-floor corridor, glimpsed a half-open door and through it he saw Oscar with his arms around the maid, or rather . . .

Maigret's eyes gleamed. This was surprising, although not entirely. He should have guessed that, in such a family, there wasn't anything sensational to be expected.

The picture of the two bachelors became clearer. Émile was chaste, but Oscar had passions. Cautious, afraid of the unforeseen, he was happy to satisfy them with Babette, who had nothing scary about her.

If it weren't for his brother, might he not be capable of marrying the maid? Perhaps! In any case, if she played her cards right . . .

And was that not the reason that Babette took the liberty of raising her voice to Françoise?

But who had sent Émile the threatening letter?

And would someone really dare to do the deed?

Lunch was a little more appetizing than the previous evening's dinner. It was Sunday! There was a starter of herring fillets, radishes and potato salad, followed by leg of lamb with beans, cheese and a cherry tart, of which Émile helped himself to the biggest slice.

Perhaps to save her mother from another scene, Éliane had reluctantly slipped on a dress, a simple white-linen dress, beneath which she must have been naked, because, when she stood up in the sunlight, her whole body could be seen through it.

The truth is that, because of that detail, Maigret barely noticed what went on during the meal. Éliane was just in front of him, on the terrace where the table had been set. And, my word, he thought, somewhat enviously, of the lucky young man who had stolen into the house at night and must have had a delectable time.

When coffee was served, Émile suddenly spoke, with an unexpected solemnity. Getting to his feet, he looked as if he wanted to make a speech, and it was indeed almost a speech, which contained all the feelings that underlay the relations among this outrageous family:

'I don't need to remind you of the threatening letter I received, which is the reason why Inspector Maigret is here today. I have no illusions about your love for me! When one is the head of a family and shoulders all the responsibilities . . .'

Because he was the eldest, as Maigret had found out that morning; Oscar had come into the world a few minutes after his brother.

'All the same, the fact is that, whether you like it or not, I insist on taking every precaution. The letter states that the murder will be committed before six o'clock this evening . . .'

Françoise, as usual, seemed to be fighting back perpetual tears. Oscar stared fixedly at Maigret. Éliane, her eyes half closed in the sunshine, was probably dreaming of sensual delights, while her brother's nostrils quivered in the way the nostrils of drug addicts desperate for a fix do.

Babette must have been in the doorway. Maigret hadn't seen her. Émile said to her:

'Come in! You're not in the way. Quite the opposite, because you're part of the family. I don't know what Inspector Maigret is planning. I don't know yet what precautions the police have taken to avert a tragedy. As far as I'm concerned, I thought that the safest way to prevent the murder is for us to stay together until six o'clock this evening.'

He glared at them defiantly, and seemed to be saying:

'Whether you like it or not, that's how it will be! Too bad for whichever one of you plotted my death!'

The response was as comical as it was unexpected, because it came from Babette, who exclaimed:

'What about my washing-up?'

'You can do it this evening.'

Éliane shot Maigret a quick glance. Their eyes met. She must have read his mind, because she blushed slightly.

As for Henri, he had turned pale, perhaps at the prospect of being deprived of cocaine, which he didn't dare take in front of everyone.

And Françoise sighed:

'Do you suspect us, Émile?'

'I suspect no one and I suspect everyone. The entire family will stay on this terrace. Babette will bring everything we need to make tea. I think Inspector Maigret can only approve these basic measures . . .'

Inspector Maigret did indeed approve! Why not? It made his job easier, saved him from having to run around all over the place to check what each of them was doing.

'What are we going to do for hours on end?' sighed Oscar.

And his brother replied bitterly:

'What do you usually do?'

Éliane couldn't help joking, as she looked at the radiant blue sky:

'Supposing it rains?'

Her uncle merely glared at her.

Too bad for the young man on the train who was going to row past the garden in his varnished canoe again and again in vain! Could he not content himself with what he'd had the previous night?

Maigret was almost beginning to enjoy himself. Leaning back in his wicker chair, he filled his pipe, tapping it with his index finger, fumbled in his pocket for matches, didn't find any, and stood up.

'What are you looking for?' asked Émile Grosbois.

'Matches . . .'

'I'll have some brought out . . . Please make sure that, after this, no one has to get up again. I apologize for being so uncompromising, but I'd like to point out that it's my life that's at stake!'

Less than fifty metres away, the railway line crossed the garden and from time to time a train went by, making a deafening racket, its foul-smelling smoke engulfing the house for a few moments.

No doubt the place had been built before the railway line. And no doubt too the compulsory purchase of a piece of their land had brought the family a tidy sum.

'Would you like a drink, inspector?'

Émile asked him this as if he were certain that the answer would be negative.

Maigret deliberately replied:

'Well, if we have to stay put for hours, I wouldn't be averse to having something to drink.'

Then Émile gave Babette the key to the cellar, saying:

'Bring a bottle of brandy: the one that's been opened and is on the shelf on the left . . .'

It was hot. Families were picnicking all along the banks of the Seine and satiated men stretched out in the long grass, a handkerchief or a newspaper over their face, looking forward to a delightful nap.

'Don't you have any games to play?' asked Maigret with irony, looking around at his companions.

Françoise shyly replied:

'There's a Pope Joan game but I don't know if it's complete . . .'

The wait began, the wait, in other words, for the death of Émile Grosbois, who sat ramrod straight in his garden chair and whose fierce gaze flitted constantly from one person to another.

3

Maigret looked at his watch. It was two o'clock precisely, which meant there were four hours to get through, sitting almost as still as on a train journey, only without the glimpses of the passing countryside, which remained obstinately the same, or the pleasures of conversation.

Despite his outer calm, you could tell that Émile Grosbois was sick with fear and, as the time went by, he became increasingly withdrawn, as if to give fate less to grab on to.

Françoise had brought out her sewing. You could tell she was a woman capable of spending her life doing chores and of finding a sort of delight in her own unhappiness.

Every five minutes, she would raise her head and sigh, gaze at each person around her with a hangdog look, sigh again and resume her sewing.

Sometimes, too, she would utter a few words to herself, as do women who spend many hours in solitude.

'I can't believe the world is so wicked!'

What was she talking about? Who? The murderer or Émile Grosbois?

Then, a little later:

'No one would dare come in with the police here . . .'

Babette, meanwhile, was furious at having been dragged away from her kitchen. She had been told to sit down, but, for at least an hour, she'd remained on her feet, in protest, upright as a statue, the embodiment of discontent.

Éliane had been more sensible. Taking the cushions from the empty chairs, she'd scattered them in a corner of the terrace and was lying in the sun, her eyes closed.

Her brother was less philosophical, and he was the one who worried Maigret. He had missed his fix and was starting to become restless, twitching nervously, and he could well have a fit later.

Then there was Oscar, who would have liked to start a conversation.

'May I tell you what I think? I'm not an expert in these matters, like Inspector Maigret. But common sense alone tells us that we are all mistaking a prank for reality . . .'

A frosty look from his brother. A sharper look from Maigret.

'Because, in short, what is this about? An almost childish letter that was nothing more than . . . pure fancy! Do murderers generally warn their victims in advance? Let's stay together here until six o'clock, since that's what we've been asked to do, but . . . let's not over-dramatize the situation, otherwise, later, we'll be forced to laugh at ourselves . . .'

'Are you the one who's being threatened?' snapped his brother.

Oscar replied, laughing:

'Well, I am almost as much as you! From a distance, it's barely possible to tell us apart. And since the murderer, if he does exist, will be shooting from a distance—'

Maigret broke in gently:

'Why are you talking about shooting?'

And Oscar, taken aback:

'But . . . I don't know . . . A murder is generally carried out with a revolver, or a gun . . .'

Confused, he mumbled:

'Because I don't suppose someone will come on to this terrace holding a knife to stab my brother.'

Émile winced, uncrossed his legs and crossed them the other way. A sigh from Françoise.

Half past two . . . Three o'clock . . . Éliane had fallen asleep, in the white dress that hugged her curves and which the breeze occasionally caused to flutter, revealing a glimpse of her tanned thighs.

A train . . .

Then, on the Seine, a tug and its barges . . .

Suddenly, at half past three, an unexpected move by Émile, proving that he really was frightened. With jerky movements that showed he had been resisting the temptation for a long time, he got up and poured himself a full glass of brandy.

His brother was flabbergasted, and so was his sister. He scowled at them and said:

'Another two and a half hours . . . !'

Shortly afterwards, beads of sweat glistened on his forehead and he bit his lower lip.

'Do you really think I couldn't have done my washing-up?'

Oscar gestured to Babette to be quiet and Maigret

smiled at the thought of the scene that morning that had finally revealed the other Grosbois' vice to him.

On the Seine, for all those who were out canoeing, sailing, or happily swimming, for the anglers watching closely for their float to quiver and for those enjoying a nap in the reeds, the hours must have seemed horribly short.

On the terrace of the Grosbois house, the minutes dragged on relentlessly, dripping one after the other like at night the constant dripping of a tap that hasn't been properly turned off.

The Lord knows that in the course of his career, Maigret had seen all sorts of phenomena and it was hard to surprise him!

But in this case, he was not just surprised, but sickened, horrified.

It seemed to him that these people, among whom chance had placed him, were deliberately ruining beautiful materials, a beautiful life, infinite possibilities.

Could Oscar, for instance, not have found other pleasures than those dispensed with contempt by the indifferent Babette?

Could Henri not have been a normal, carefree young man and enjoyed the best days of his life?

Only Éliane . . .

'They're idiots!' he concluded. 'It is so rare to meet someone who knows how to enjoy life!'

In the meantime, there was, within the family circle, someone who had planned to kill! Would this someone carry out their threat regardless?

Now another thought occurred to Maigret, a terrifying

thought! If the murder didn't take place, would Émile, the next day, rush to see his municipal councillor or perhaps someone even higher up! He would claim that his life was still under threat and would obtain . . .

Yes . . . ! If the murder didn't take place, there was a strong likelihood that Maigret would be tied for an indeterminate time to the movements of the man and of his dreadful family!

'Let's hope . . .'

Maigret wasn't wishing for Émile's death, but he did want something to happen that would put an end to the man's anxieties!

'One question,' he said out loud. 'Is there a train at around six p.m.?'

'No! There's a fast train at 4.47 and a local train at 7.05 . . .'

It was just an idea! Rather a stupid idea, in short, because to shoot Émile Grosbois required him to be in his garden just when the train was passing through . . .

'I'd thought of that too!' sighed Françoise. 'I was even going to suggest we go inside. Don't you find it a bit chilly?'

'Not at all!'

It was hot. Maigret felt a little flustered as he contemplated the downy golden hairs on Éliane's neck, which was covered in a light dew.

What a waste of time!

And all because of a man, or rather two disagreeable men!

At four o'clock, or shortly after, Émile poured some more brandy and, since he wasn't used to it, it was obvious from his eyes that he was getting drunk.

'Shall I make the tea?' offered Babette, who was visibly bored.

'Not yet. We had a late lunch . . .'

'What about dinner? Do you think dinner will be ready, with all your nonsense?'

'Quiet!' said Émile's dull voice.

'Fine! We'll keep quiet! But don't complain later if . . .'

'Quiet!'

'No need to shout so loud. I've never seen . . .'

'Silence!' he yelled, sitting up straight. 'You're forgetting that I might be about to die. I know you'd all be pleased. Yes, I know it and you barely bother to hide it. But . . .'

He suddenly let rip, perhaps under the influence of the alcohol.

'. . . the inspector is here, do you understand? So the murderer won't get away with it! You may be bored . . . It's a wasted afternoon . . . But you have to admit that it's better than a corpse . . . Quiet!'

Oscar looked at Maigret and rolled his eyes.

'Completely mad!' he seemed to be signalling.

Françoise trembled at each outburst, as if she had been threatened. Éliane raised her head, batted her eyelashes, smoothed her dress down a little over her thighs, which were almost fully revealed by the breeze, and, indifferent, resumed her comfortable position and tried to go back to sleep.

'I will not tolerate that, in our house . . .'

Émile, unable to find any contradiction to stoke his anger, was going to have to calm down, when, to the amazement of everyone except Maigret, who had been expecting it for a few minutes, Henri stood up, ashen, his lips trembling.

His nostrils had been pinched for a while, and his fingers were twitching.

'You're mad!' he yelled. 'Do you hear? You may be my uncle, but nothing will stop me telling you that you're mad and a brute! As for me, I won't stay a minute longer in this house! I've had enough . . . ! Enough . . . ! Enough . . . !'

His mother couldn't believe her eyes, and sat numb with shock. Émile looked at his nephew and wondered whether he was out of his mind.

'Henri . . . !' he shouted.

'Damn you!'

'Henri . . . ! I must . . . I forbid . . .'

Too late! The young man, who had already left the terrace, was lurching across the garden, probably continuing his tirade in an undertone.

Émile seemed to be on the verge of running after him and the scene would have then ended up becoming ridiculous. Instead, he said:

'Inspector, you are a witness. I'm asking you to arrest that young man, to stop him from leaving . . .'

Maigret did not move.

'I demand that you . . .'

'I'm sorry,' muttered Maigret calmly. 'We are in Seine-et-Oise here, you know. The chief explained to you yesterday we are outside the jurisdiction of the Police Judiciaire and my role is restricted to protecting you. Even in Paris, I would have no grounds for arresting your nephew because he said "Damn you" . . .'

'Very well . . . ! Very well . . . ! Very well . . . !'

He was foaming at the mouth. Without thinking, he poured himself another drink and, forgetting perhaps that it was brandy, took a large mouthful that almost choked him.

'Babette . . . ! Babette . . . !'

'I'm here, monsieur.'

'Make the tea . . . Everything's on the terrace, isn't it . . . ? I don't want anyone else to leave . . .'

He had to mop his face, get his breath back. Then he looked at his watch and mopped his face again, because it was nearly five o'clock.

'Calm down,' cautioned his brother.

Émile gave him a filthy look, his mouth half-opening for a new outburst of anger but then closing again without his having said a word.

'If only a person could get some sleep around here!' sighed Éliane, her eyes still shut.

On the table that had not been cleared after lunch, Babette had lit a spirit stove to boil water for the tea. Maigret smoked continuously, swearing never to accept missions like this ever again and to be wary from now on of rag merchants and unmarried twins.

'If anything were to happen to me, inspector, I must tell you . . .'

Maigret almost blurted out, like Henri:

'Damn you!'

He didn't. To his cost.

'. . . that you will be answerable to public opinion for—'

'. . . for your death. I know! But let me point out that

you're the one who, without consulting me, took all these precautions—'

'Are they useless?'

'I didn't say that.'

'So what would you have done?'

'The question isn't relevant, given that there are only fifty minutes left.'

The more the hour approached, the more anxious, tense, wary and aggressive Émile became.

'When I think that someone in my family . . .'

'Why necessarily someone in your family?'

'Because they hate me! Because they've always hated me!'

He was like those beings who have acted tough all their lives and who, as they near death, lose all sense of shame, beg, and are ready to confess to the first person they come across.

'A simple detail! I've thought long and hard about the matter! The letter was made from words and letters cut from the newspapers we regularly receive at home . . .'

'I imagine other people receive them?'

Maigret had truly had enough. His contempt was so great that he felt capable, like Henri, of leaving before the end of this sickening wait.

'The sugar, Françoise!'

'It's inside the house . . .'

'Go and fetch it . . . Or rather, no . . . ! Inspector, go with her . . . No . . . !'

He no longer knew what precautions to take. He didn't want a single person to go into the house. He didn't want to go himself. Nor did he want to be without Maigret's help, just in case . . .

'We'll have our tea without sugar . . .'

'But . . .' protested his brother.

'Quiet! Am I or am I not the one who's supposed to get killed?'

Human cowardice in all its manifestations erupted within him, while all around there was nothing but spinelessness. A true devotee of the tearful life, Françoise poured the tea and was still sniffing.

The only person who had stayed more or less calm was Oscar, who took advantage of a lull to say:

'I'm certain nothing will happen. I'm the one who was right: it's a prank . . .'

And, to his brother, who was glowering at him:

'You'd have done better to listen to me and go to the mountains where I've found a good place. A few weeks' rest . . . Besides, it's not too late . . .'

Twenty past five. People were still bathing in the Seine. Éliane, her eyes still closed, her chest rising each time she breathed in, was perhaps dreaming of the joys she was being deprived of today.

'More?'

'Leave me alone . . .'

As he had done the previous day, Émile selected a pill from his box, in which only three remained, and washed it down with a mouthful of tea.

'You'll make yourself ill as a result of believing yourself ill,' reprimanded his brother. 'Whereas a little rest . . .'

Why the devil was he so determined to get his brother away from Paris? Why was he insisting that he needed a rest cure in a convalescent home, a cure that could very well end up with his being sent to a lunatic asylum?

Was it because of Babette? Did he want more freedom? Had she persuaded him to marry her and was he afraid Émile would veto it?

Instead of sugar, Maigret poured brandy into his tea, because he almost felt like getting drunk to take his mind off all this unpleasantness.

Half past five . . .

He was surprised at how calm Émile Grosbois was and he watched him and saw how pale he was in his chair, one hand on his chest, his pupils dilated.

'Does your brother have a heart condition?' he asked Oscar in an undertone.

'He believes so. That's why he takes medication . . .'

At that moment, they heard a regular wheezing sound coming from Émile, who was gradually sliding down in his chair.

Maigret rushed over.

'An emetic . . . Quick . . . !' he shouted.

'We don't have any . . .'

'Anything to make him vomit . . . ! Wait . . . A chicken or pigeon feather . . .'

Émile was no longer moving. He was ashen, not even a tremor, no sign of life.

'A spoon . . . ! Quick, dammit . . . !'

And Maigret promptly set to work, prising open the rag

merchant's teeth with the spoon and ramming the feather Babette had brought him down his throat.

'What the hell . . . !' he exclaimed.

It was his turn to be the only one to speak. To give orders:

'Go on, throw up . . . ! Throw up if you don't want to die . . . !'

He may have despised the victim, but he was still extremely anxious, and he barely noticed the astonishment on Oscar's face.

'Support him . . . ! His chest forward . . . Yes, like that . . . Don't let go, damned fool!'

These are minutes during which there is not time to consider, or even to think. One acts instinctively, by reflex.

Maigret's reflexes were good, luckily for Émile Grosbois, who eventually ceased to look like a pillar of salt and came to with a retch and finally vomited up all he could.

'A doctor . . . ! You, Éliane . . . ! Run and fetch a doctor . . .'

Six o'clock! The bells of a tiny nearby church rang out ironically.

'Keep tickling the back of his throat so that he brings up everything that's in his stomach . . .'

It was almost an act of vengeance to see Émile Grosbois, bent double, held in a solid grip and retching, with long dribbles of saliva under his chin.

4

'So? Your weekend?'

The superintendent, in the sunlight, was stroking his white goatee and smiling mischievously at a grumpy Maigret.

'Next time you'll be so kind as to send someone else on this type of mission. It's all very well saving people, but preferably when they're deserving! But as long as they are—'

'Who are you talking about?'

'The entire family!'

'Without exception?'

'Let's say, perhaps, with the exception of a beautiful girl who . . . and even then! Women shouldn't be allowed to play at the Temptation of Saint Anthony for an entire Sunday afternoon! When a woman has a body like that, she should conceal it, otherwise . . .'

'The threatening letter?'

'I was certain from the beginning. Sent by the brother, Oscar, of course! He'd been attempting to get rid of his older brother for a long time by trying to persuade him to go for a cure in the mountains. And it was he who, on the pretext of protesting about the medicines Émile was taking, kept thrusting medical books under his nose. Do you follow?'

'Umm...'

'You can't understand if you don't know the family... In short, Oscar, at fifty something, wanted to live his life, which he couldn't do while he was under his brother's thumb... He said to himself that, by scaring him, he'd finally get him to leave Paris, which would have allowed him to indulge in his little debaucheries with Babette, and probably marry her...'

'It may be very clear to you, but for me—'

'It doesn't matter...! Oscar confessed... I was sure he wouldn't take the joke any further, that he'd never make an attempt on his brother's life... Unfortunately, like many pranks, this one almost ended in a tragedy, because it gave someone ideas... A pathetic fellow, the nephew, raised in that madhouse, hyper from an addiction to cocaine, torn in different directions, crazy, yelled at all day long—'

'I'm finding it harder and harder to follow you!'

'I'll try and be more precise in my report, but this one won't be easy to write. In other words, young Henri, informed of the threat hanging over his uncle, said to himself that he could very well carry it out... Mind you, everyone in that household would have happily done so... Do you know the paradox of the mandarin...? If Oscar, Babette, Françoise or Éliane had been given the opportunity to get rid of Émile by pressing a button...

'Henri tried to do so by putting a strong dose of cocaine in the tablets his uncle took at set times...

'He didn't have the gumption to witness his dying moments...

'The police picked him up in Paris that night, when,

scared out of his wits, he'd taken a massive amount of cocaine and collapsed in a Montmartre drinking den . . .

'That's all.'

Maigret wiped his hand across his brow, went over to the window and inhaled the morning air, taking a deep breath.

'Has he been arrested?'

'In hospital . . . The uncle hasn't lodged a complaint. He's terrified at the thought of a public hearing in the criminal courts . . .'

'So . . . ?'

'Nothing! My wife is furious! Émile threw up on my trousers, which will have to be sent to the dry cleaners, and she spent an unpleasant Sunday . . .'

He lit his pipe and grunted, between puffs, the smoke rising in the sunlight:

'Give me a likeable scoundrel . . . ! But those people . . .'

And the chief replied ironically:

'The Police Judiciaire doesn't deal only with murderers, Maigret. Don't forget the other section, the one under which you're going to file your report.'

'. . . ?'

'Investigations undertaken on behalf of private families . . .'

The chief wasn't sure he heard correctly:

'Damn!'

Because Maigret was already opening the door.

INSPECTOR MAIGRET

OTHER TITLES IN THE SERIES

MY FRIEND MAIGRET
GEORGES SIMENON

'The palm trees around the railway station were motionless, fixed in a Saharan sun . . . It really felt as if they were stepping into another world, and they were embarrassed to be entering it in the dark clothes that had been suited to the rainy streets of Paris the evening before.'

An officer from Scotland Yard is studying Maigret's methods when a call from an island off the Côte d'Azur sends the two men off to an isolated community to investigate its eccentric inhabitants.

Translated by Shaun Whiteside

www.penguin.com

INSPECTOR MAIGRET

OTHER TITLES IN THE SERIES

MAIGRET AND THE KILLER
GEORGES SIMENON

'Leaning on the banisters, Madame Maigret watched her husband going heavily downstairs . . . what the newspapers didn't know was how much energy he put into trying to understand, how much he concentrated during certain investigations. It was as if he identified with the people he was hunting and suffered the same torments as they did.'

A young man is found dead, clutching his tape recorder, just streets away from Maigret's home, leading the inspector on a disturbing trail into the mind of a killer.

Translated by Shaun Whiteside

www.penguin.com

INSPECTOR MAIGRET

OTHER TITLES IN THE SERIES

MAIGRET AND MONSIEUR CHARLES
GEORGES SIMENON

'He needed to get out of his office, soak up the atmosphere and discover different worlds with each new investigation. He needed the cafés and bars where he so often ended up waiting, at the counter, drinking a beer or a calvados depending on the circumstances. He needed to do battle patiently in his office with a suspect who refused to talk and sometimes, after hours and hours, he'd obtain a dramatic confession.'

In Simenon's final novel featuring Inspector Maigret, the famous detective reaches a pivotal moment in his career, contemplating his past and future as he delves into the Paris underworld one last time, to investigate the case of a missing lawyer.

Translated by Ros Schwartz

www.penguin.com

Other Titles in the Series

Pietr the Latvian
The Late Monsieur Gallet
The Hanged Man of Saint-Pholien
The Carter of *La Providence*
The Yellow Dog
Night at the Crossroads
A Crime in Holland
The Grand Banks Café
A Man's Head
The Dancer at the Gai-Moulin
The Two-Penny Bar
The Shadow Puppet
The Saint-Fiacre Affair
The Flemish House
The Madman of Bergerac
The Misty Harbour
Liberty Bar
Lock No. 1
Maigret
Cécile is Dead
The Cellars of the Majestic
The Judge's House
Signed, Picpus
Inspector Cadaver
Félicie
Maigret Gets Angry
Maigret in New York
Maigret's Holiday
Maigret's Dead Man
Maigret's First Case
My Friend Maigret
Maigret at the Coroner's
Maigret and the Old Lady
Madame Maigret's Friend
Maigret's Memoirs
Maigret at Picratt's
Maigret Takes a Room
Maigret and the Tall Woman

Maigret, Lognon and the Gangsters
Maigret's Revolver
Maigret and the Man on the Bench
Maigret is Afraid
Maigret's Mistake
Maigret Goes to School
Maigret and the Dead Girl
Maigret and the Minister
Maigret and the Headless Corpse
Maigret Sets a Trap
Maigret's Failure
Maigret Enjoys Himself
Maigret Travels
Maigret's Doubts
Maigret and the Reluctant Witness
Maigret's Secret
Maigret in Court
Maigret and the Old People
Maigret and the Lazy Burglar
Maigret and the Good People of Montparnasse
Maigret and the Saturday Caller
Maigret and the Tramp
Maigret's Anger
Maigret and the Ghost
Maigret Defends Himself
Maigret's Patience
Maigret and the Nahour Case
Maigret's Pickpocket
Maigret Hesitates
Maigret in Vichy
Maigret's Childhood Friend
Maigret and the Killer
Maigret and the Wine Merchant
Maigret's Madwoman
Maigret and the Loner
Maigret and the Informer
Maigret and Monsieur Charles

www.penguin.com